Eagle Ray

by

Devin Riggh

Eagle Ray

Cover Design by Sean Lanning: www.iamsrlmedia.com

ISBN-13: 978-1535385268

ISBN-10: 153538526X

Author's Note: For your convenience, a glossary of sailing and diving terminology has been included at the end of this novel.

Prologue

My mother blames my condition on a witch. As of the moment that I'm writing this, the world record for a human holding his breath is 11 minutes and 35 seconds. The longest that I have held my breath was four hours. When I resumed breathing it was due to boredom, and not the need for air. The deepest recorded breath-hold dive was to 702 feet. So far, breath-hold divers are limited to a depth of around and about 700 feet. Depending on the individual, the pressure being exerted on a human ribcage at that depth tends to compress the chest and lungs to the point that the lung walls touch one another, and then the alveoli rupture, causing pulmonary edema and death. I dive alone, so for safety's sake, I make it a rule to go no deeper than 600 feet. I have no idea how long I can stay at that depth. I don't want you to think that I'm a boastful person. This ability doesn't make me superior in any way. It's simply an accident of birth and a biological anomaly. Concealing the ability is a never-ending effort, but it has saved my life once or twice.

My name is Jamie Bonifacio and my family is from Puerto Rico. I was born on the island of Culebra, into a family of fishermen. Shortly before I was born, my father was bringing in a record number of fish when others were bringing in almost nothing. The Guzman family who lived nearby also had a fishing operation, but things were not going well for them. The matriarch of the family was Doña Maria Theresa Guzman. Doña Maria was a priestess of the religion called Santeria. Doña Maria believed that my mother was using magic to help my dad catch most of the fish in the area, thereby cheating the other fishermen out of their fair share of the bounty of the sea. The truth was that the waters had been overfished and that my father knew the location of the few spots where the remaining fish could be harvested.

One day when my mom was pregnant with me, Doña Maria showed up at our front door. I was told that she said something to the effect of, "Whatsoever you sow, that shall you also reap. You have sown to your flesh, and so shall your flesh reap corruption! You take all of the fish! Your child shall be a fish!" My parents laughed off the encounter with Doña Maria, until three months later, when I was born. I was delivered at home by Doctor Carlos Bengoa. In addition to being an OB-GYN, Doctor Carlos has a deep and abiding fascination with crypto-zoology.

That's probably why he made a point of becoming friends with my parents and me. I must have looked like a monster when I was born. For one thing, my hands and feet were webbed. There was also webbing between my legs. I imagine that I actually did resemble a fish, or maybe a manatee. Dr. Carlos said that palmate is the word that biologists use to describe an animal with webbed hands or feet. I was a very palmate newborn.

At the request of my parents, Dr. Carlos surgically removed the skin that formed the webbing. He did as well as he was able, but the scars are still noticeable. I make a point of wearing long pants when I go shopping or out to eat, or to other public places. Still, I spend a lot of time in swim trunks and people occasionally notice the scars. When that happens their faces show in turn confusion, recognition, revulsion, and embarrassment. Then, they quickly look away. Only young children ask me about the scars. I tell them that I used to be a merman, but that I had an operation to make me a human. It's not entirely untrue. Sometimes, I wish that I still had webbed feet and hands, because it would probably make me a more efficient swimmer. I can do without the webbing that connected my legs together. I have a driver's license, but not a car, so I ride a bike most everywhere I go.

Dr. Carlos has been a good friend to me and my mom. He comes to see me twice a year for a check-up, at no charge. Dr. Carlos discovered my ability when I was an infant. Apparently, I would stop breathing for long periods of time, which understandably alarmed my parents. Dr. Carlos assured them that I would be fine, but admitted that he was unsure how such a thing could be possible. He said that my ability to hold my breath is most likely due to a profound mutation of my Erythropoietin Receptor gene. That particular gene dictates the body's ability to produce the red blood cells that carry oxygen to the tissues. That also explains why my skin tone changes from well-tanned to bright red whenever I'm angry or embarrassed. The mutation also seems to allow me to run and swim longer than most people.

There's one other thing that's odd about me. I have a very keen sense of smell. Strong smells, such as perfume can cause me to feel unexpected emotions and sometimes experience vivid memories. When I was a child, cigarette smoke would send me into tears. As I've aged, my reaction to scents has reduced in intensity. I asked Dr. Carlos about it a couple of years ago, and he said that my heightened sense of smell might have something to do with increased availability of oxygen. But, he said that my reaction to scents was unrelated. He said that the olfactory nerves are hardwired to a part of the brain called the paleocortex. So, Dr. Carlos sent me for an MRI that confirmed that the paleocortex in my brain was larger than normal. He also said that my mutation might be a sort of evolutionary hiccup.

Shortly after I was born, Dad decided that we should leave PR and move to the mainland. He stopped being a fisherman and went to school to be a commercial diver. In his new job, Dad spent most of his time at sea, working on oil rigs in many different places around the world. He wanted to settle someplace that would make his time with his family feel like a vacation, so he moved our family to Sarasota, Florida. He said that he had picked Sarasota because he'd read that it had the most beautiful white-sand beach in America, on Siesta Key.

Dad was a talented, hard-working guy. His name was Salvador. People called him Sal. Whenever I want to be reminded of him, I read that short story by Somerset Maugham,

Salvatore. My dad loved the ocean, and I think that I love the ocean even more than he did. Unfortunately, Dad passed away three years ago. It was an accident at work. Dad's life insurance policy paid off our house, and there was enough left over for Mom to get her LPN license. Aside from my genetic mutation, I was a regular guy who had friends, went to school, went fishing, and did all of the other things that young people do, until early one summer when everything went south.

Chapter One

May 13th had been the last day of tenth grade, and after nine months of being talked at, I was ready to get back on the water. I'd spent the weekend prepping and by the morning of Monday the 16th I was motoring across Sarasota Bay in my sailboat. She's a twenty-two foot Catalina called Eagle Ray. I named her for the Spotted Eagle Ray, the most graceful and beautiful animal in the world. I saw a pair of them once when I was freediving out in the Gulf of Mexico. They were obviously mature specimens, because their body length, not counting their tails, was at least eight feet. Their wingspan was a bit more. Something about the way the Catalina's sails catch air when I tack or jibe reminds me of an Eagle Ray winging its way through the water. I bought the boat for $1600 of my own money, which I'd earned by cleaning boat hulls and performing other boat maintenance services.

Sarasota Bay is full of sailboats at anchor that need their hulls scraped every ninety days or so. Luckily, no one but me wants to do the job, because the people who swing on the hook in Sarasota Bay usually can't afford to pay what the hull cleaning companies charge. There are at least fifty boats in the bay at any given time, and I charge between $40 and $60 per boat for a hull cleaning, which is a bargain. I've started making a name for myself and sometimes cruisers who I've never met pull into Sarasota Bay just to have me clean their hulls. I can clean an average of three hulls per day. I usually work 60 or 70 days during summer breaks and on weekends during the school year. You can do the math if you want, but it suffices to say that I do okay.

I started cleaning hulls when I was thirteen, right after my dad died. Back then, I would paddle out to the boats on a kayak that I'd bought at a garage sale and ask around for hulls. My reputation for speedy, reliable and affordable work grew and so did my clientele. It wasn't long until I'd earned enough to buy a real boat. I don't have to ask around for work anymore, because everyone in the bay has my business card. My only complaint about my job is that I have to find a way to keep my hair out of my face underwater. I like my hair long, but it washes back and forth in the surge and I can't see well enough to do my work. Last year, I cut it short for the summer, but it took forever to grow back. This year, I bought a light neoprene hood and it's worked fairly well. It's not perfect, but it's better than the alternative.

My boat was named Triple Decker when I bought it. The man who sold it to me was named Decker and he said that the "triple" referred to himself, his wife, and his child. I changed the name as soon as possible. A superstitious sailor will tell you that it's extremely bad luck to rename a boat. According to some, Poseidon keeps track of each and every vessel on the high seas by recording its name in the Ledger of the Deep. Recently, I've learned that by tradition, if you must rename a boat you can only do it once and you must do that immediately after the first time that you sail her. It's crucial that there be no trace of the original name left anywhere onboard. It can't be on maintenance records, or life rings, or anything else. Also, you're supposed to pour champagne into the sea during a ceremony in which you pay homage to Poseidon. I'm too young to buy champagne, and the whole thing seemed a little silly to me, so I just repainted my hull with white marine paint and applied some vinyl letters to spell out the new name. Later, Murray, an artist, client and friend of mine insisted on painting the boat's name and a representation of a

3

spotted eagle ray on the port and starboard stern quarters. It's an attractive decoration and it's become a sort of company logo. After he'd finished the work, Murray insisted on performing a ceremony of some kind. He stood at the bow pulpit and poured some Ron Rico over the side of my boat and said, "Oh, mighty Poseidon! We humbly ask your forgiveness for obliging your secretary to update your books! Sorry for the imposition! It's just that Triple Decker is a dumb name for a 22 foot sloop! Rub-a-dub-dub, protect this leaky tub! Amen!" It was obvious that significantly more of the rum went into Murray than went across the bow. I don't think that was a proper way to petition a deity for protection, but then again, what do I know?

It's funny that I happened to mention Murray, because his boat was the first stop of the day. He owns a 1984 Formosa 51, named Kick-Back. Kick-Back could be really beautiful if he attended to details, such as keeping a fresh finish on the teak and polishing the bright-work. She's an aft-cabin ketch with a 14' beam, and two heads. She's basically a two-bedroom apartment that floats. The fact that he doesn't like to work on his boat has made Murray one of my best customers. His boat is a $60 hull and he hires me to scrape it regularly. He knows that it's much cheaper to keep the hull clean, than to move it to a haul-out yard for a bottom-job.

I like to stay under power if I'm navigating close to other boats. Murray was on deck when I pulled up, reversed the engine to stop my forward progress, and killed my outboard. I tossed Murray my bow line, which he secured to an aft horn cleat. I then tossed him my stern line, which he tied to a fore horn cleat. Then, we secured forward and aft spring lines. Murray said, "Hey man, thanks for coming out. The bottom doesn't look too bad from up top, but I wanted a professional opinion." The last time that I'd cleaned the hull had been in February, so I knew that Kick-Back would be thick with barnacles. I said, "It looks alright, I guess, for swinging on the hook. But, I don't think that you'd want to go far without a cleaning." He said, "You read my mind. I've been thinking about making a run down to the Thousand Islands." The Thousand Islands are located in the St. Lawrence River on the border with Canada. I knew that he actually meant the Ten Thousand Islands National Wildlife Refuge, which is located about a hundred miles south of Sarasota, in the Everglades. I didn't correct him. What's the point? Correcting equals belittling and that comes with a cost. You might not think that words have much power, but they do. People talk. If I got a reputation as a smart-mouth, people would stop recommending me and my business would dry up faster than a jellyfish on the beach. Besides that, when I've belittled people in the past, it didn't make me feel smarter or better, it just made me feel like a jerk.

Murray had decided to open his wallet and an open wallet smells like opportunity, so I said, "I know you want your boat to look nice for the ladies when you go cruising. Why don't you hire me to refinish your teak?" He looked around at his railings and said, "Nah. I like the wood this way. It's kind of rustic looking." My face must have betrayed my disappointment, because he added, "I'm sorry Jamie, but I'm on a tight budget this month." I sensed that it would be a kindness to change the subject. I asked, "So, why did you name this boat Kick-Back?" He said, "The name came with the boat. I like it though, because it sums up my philosophy. I'm kicked-back and takin' it easy. Stress is for people who don't appreciate that life is short, you know?" I agreed, "I can't argue with that. Who did you buy her from?" He said, "You know the Sheriff's confiscated property auction? I picked her up cheap there. She'd belonged to some guy who used to work for the county."

I donned my wetsuit, gloves, neoprene boots, fins and mask. I also put on a weight belt with four pounds of lead to compensate for the buoyancy of the wetsuit. I go through a lot of gear in this job because it gets torn up by barnacles. You have to wear neoprene when you clean a hull. If you get scraped by a barnacle you can get a bacterial infection that can kill you if you don't get antibiotics right away. My mask and fins do better than the neoprene, but it seems as though I change them more than I change my underwear. I never seem to be able to find a mask that fits exactly right, or fins that feel exactly right. It's become almost an obsession, and I hate to admit it, but I've wasted quite a bit of money pursuing the perfect fit.

That day, I was using a yellow Mares mask and matching yellow Mares full foot fins. They aren't as fast as some of my other fins, but they're comfortable and I don't need neoprene boots with them, just some fin socks. Fin socks are easier to clean than boots, so that's worth a lot to me. Sometimes, if the water is really calm, I just wear my old Chuck Taylor's and forget the fins. While I was working, I found myself fiddling with the nose pocket of my mask because that one part of the mask is too large for my face. There always seems to be something that's not quite right about my gear.

I slid my legs over the gunwale, pointed my fin tips straight down, and placed my left hand over my mask to prevent it riding up or off of my face when I entered the water. I pushed away with my right hand and raised it above my head to minimize water resistance. For years, I've been tweaking my entry with the goal of entering the water without a splash or a sound. There's no practical advantage to doing this, but I consider myself a professional and I pride myself on doing things in a workmanlike manner. Lately, my customers have been commenting about it. They say things like, "Oh! I didn't realize that you'd gone in the water!" I think that I'm getting close to a soundless entry.

When I'm cleaning boats, I have to remember to surface occasionally to simulate the need for air. If I didn't come up every five minutes or so, then a client would naturally assume that I had drowned. I would then have to explain how I'd stayed down so long, and that's a conversation that I'd prefer to avoid. I don't see any advantage in letting people know about my condition. Besides, if people thought that I was a freak, it might cost me business. I cleaned the side of the hull opposite my boat. Then, Murray and I moved my boat to the opposite side of his, and I finished the job. I tossed my gear aboard Eagle Ray. Murray handed me three twenties, and said, "I'll see you when I see you." I didn't know if Murray was really going cruising. Boat people tend to go where they want, when they want. For example, Kick-Back disappeared one day early last year, and I didn't see her again for six months. When I talked to Murray again he said, "Yeah, Dude. You know, my feet got itchy and I decided to make a run down to Cozumel and do a little diving."

Most of my business is transacted with the folks who anchor their vessels just south of the marina near downtown Sarasota. That particular day, I had two more jobs after Kick-Back, but they were smaller $40 hulls. One of the hulls was a small, ugly house-boat that took me all of twenty minutes to clean. I felt the urge to apologize for charging the $40 minimum, but I stifled it. This is my business, I provide a valuable service, and I

9

deserve to be compensated for my time as well as my effort. I would have liked to have kept working all day, but I had no more appointments, so I knocked off around one in the afternoon. As I motored past the marina, it occurred to me that I could make three times as much per hull if I could get established there. Unfortunately, that's impossible for someone of my age and means. The marinas require that anyone working on their premises have a two-million dollar liability insurance policy. Even if I were old enough to sign a contract, I couldn't afford the insurance premiums. It was a stupid thing to say, but it popped out of my mouth anyway, "One day, I'm going to own that place."

I glanced up at the wind indicator on the masthead and found that I was in luck. The wind was from the south-east which meant that I could run before the wind instead of burning fuel. I turned Eagle Ray head-to-wind and then killed the outboard. I started to hoist the halyard, but it came off of the topmost pulley. That left me with a decision to make. I could either motor to the marina and step the mast, or climb the mast and fix it here. The mast of a Catalina 22 isn't designed to be climbed. It's designed to be easily stepped by a couple of people, or by one person with the right equipment. But I've never liked to ask for help with things like that. So, soon after I bought the boat, I made a climbing tool by tying together the ends of a short length of a car's seatbelt. I loop the seatbelt around the mast and this provides friction and a hand-hold for my right hand. Using the tool, my bare feet and the hollow of my left arm, I can shinny up the mast in a few seconds. Some of my friends have won bets from people who didn't believe that I could do it. I have to slow down about halfway up the mast to undo the seatbelt tool and reattach it above the shroud spreader.

After a brief cost-benefit analysis, I decided to effect an onsite repair, rather than burn fuel. Once I reached the top of the mast, I reset the halyard into the pulley and climbed back down. I hoisted the halyard, and then gave it a couple turns on the winch and cleated it off. I eased the boom topping lift just a little, and adjusted the outhaul, Cunningham, and boom-vang until it felt like it would be well trimmed after the mainsail had filled. I said to myself, "Helms a-lee," and then pulled the tiller hard to port and Eagle Ray caught the wind and I was underway. I hauled in the jib sheet and the self-furling jib rolled out nice and neat. I adjusted the mainsail until the telltale ribbons confirmed that the mainsail was in trim. I prettied up the jib lines and pointed my bow toward the Ringling Causeway.

The sailing club where I berth my boat is located just north of the causeway. The sailing club is a bird watcher's paradise. There's an osprey we call Oscar that perches on one of the taller wooden pylons. It's always fun to watch him dive into the water and come up with a fish. Oscar is my favorite, but there are many other birds as well, such as pelicans and snowy egrets. I was nearing the sailing club when I saw my buddy Zinx piloting his cabin cruiser toward the public boat ramp. Zinx is a marine mechanic and salver who I met when I needed my outboard repaired. He got the nickname Zinx because he's zealous about reminding people to replace their sacrificial anodes, which are more commonly known as zincs. I don't know his real name. By the time that I felt comfortable enough to ask, we were such good friends that admitting I didn't know his name would have been both insulting and embarrassing. I drop by his shop every couple of weeks. People give him perfectly good used boat parts that he doesn't really need. If I see something that I can make use of, he lets me have it. Neither Zinx nor I like to see useful things go into a landfill.

I waved and when he saw me he yelled, "Jamie! Heave to!" I assumed a close-hauled course and then tacked and heaved-to. I furled my jib and mainsail and hung the fenders from my boat's lifeline. Soon after, he pulled alongside. I asked him how his day of fishing had been. He said, "It was awesome, man. I got my limit on grouper and hogs. In fact, I've got something for you." He reached into his cooler and handed me a hogfish. I said, "Really? Are you kidding me? Thank you, so much!" Hogfish is my favorite food. It tastes like lobster, but light and flakey. I think that it has a coconut undertone, but not everyone agrees on that point. I like to sprinkle them with a little Everglades Seasoning and slather them with butter and top them off with lime. Then, I bake them at 350 for 20 minutes. At that moment, I could not remember being happier. It was my first real day of freedom and I was going to have hogfish for dinner.

I asked, "Where's Goldie?" He said, "She's here on my boat, just watching her TV." I was confused, so I asked, "She's watching TV?" He said, "Come aboard and check this out." When

I climbed on his boat, I saw Goldie, his retriever mix poised over the live bait well. Her hindquarters were splayed out behind her and she'd laid her paws on either side of the well. Her head moved left and right as she tried to follow the movements of the darting bait fish. He said, "She's been right there all day." I thanked Zinx again for the fish and motored into my slip. After I'd tied off to the dock cleats, I washed down my boat with freshwater, flaked and stowed my mainsail, and then covered it with a canvas sail cover for protection from the sun. Sails are expensive, and nearly indispensible if you want to go sailing, so it's a good idea to take care of them.

The sailing club has a clubhouse where sailors can hang out and have a meal or a refreshing beverage. After work, I ride my bike home but I always like to have a soda and chat with whoever is around. It's a nice way to unwind and maybe line up a client. I like the atmosphere of the place. It's not a terribly old building, but it has an old feel. The walls are of good quality wood paneling and there's a pleasant salty, musty smell about the place. There's a fireplace on the southeast corner of the main room that has wood ash in the hearth, but I've never seen it used.

Even though there are picture windows in most every wall, it's always somewhat dark inside. It feels as though it was designed to be a refuge from our sub-tropical sun.

As I was walking toward the clubhouse, I saw Sid, a local charter captain standing under a sunshade, smoking his pipe. I stopped to exchange pleasantries and compare notes. I called out, "Captain Sid! Hi! How's it going?" Sid removed the pipe stem from his mouth and said, "Not too bad, Jamie. That's a nice hog you've got there. You want to sell it? I'll give you twenty bucks for it." I said, "I think not." Hogfish goes for $30 a serving if you can find it. Sid laughed and said, "You can't blame a guy for trying. How's business?" I told him, "Business is good. I only cleaned three hulls today, but I have commitments for six more already. This is only my first full day since school let out, so it'll pick up." Sid said, "That's great. I'm doing good, too. I've got more charters lined up than I can handle. I may have to hire another captain and buy another boat. In fact, you've got a job waiting on you when you get your captain's license." I said, "I don't have enough logged sea time, yet." He said, "Oh, that's right. I keep forgetting. I know that I've asked you a thousand times, but why don't you come to a Coast Guard Auxiliary meeting sometime? We're a fun bunch of people, and it would put you on a fast-track toward your six-pack. Plus, it would make you an informal member of the law enforcement community, which would cut down on the number of times that you're stopped by patrol boats." That last bit sounded really good to me. I get stopped and checked for safety equipment at least once a week, by city and county officers as well as the Coast Guard. It's always the same half-dozen officers and they never seem to recognize me or my boat. I said, "I'm not really a joiner, but just to make you happy, I'll come to a meeting."

Sid loves to complain about power-boaters, so I gave him the opportunity. "Are you still having trouble with powerboats?" Sid became animated, "Don't even get me started. Every single time I take passengers out, some idiot passes across my bow and stops us dead in the water. They don't follow the rules of the road. They don't even seem to know anything about navigational aids. Jamie, I can tell you exactly how I'm going to die. One day, I'm going to be out on the bay and some jerk is going to swamp me and my boat's going to sink and I'm going to drown. The state should require people to get a license to operate a boat. These people have more money than sense." He went on for a while. Unless Sid was a non-swimmer, it seemed unlikely that he would drown in the bay. It's ten feet at the deepest, and there are plenty of places that are less than five feet deep. In fact, I can't remember a day when I haven't seen several boats stuck on sandbars during low tide. Besides that, there are so many boats on the bay at any given time that someone would surely pick him up within a few minutes of falling overboard.

I felt the need to wrap things up. It was hot and I was thirsty and I really wanted a cold drink. I brought up the topic that traditionally punctuates our conversations. "What's the weather looking like?" Sid said, "Not good. We're looking at 20 knot winds starting a little after sundown, and continuing through tomorrow morning. It might settle down in the afternoon, but I still had to postpone my charters for tomorrow." That was bad news. If I took my boat into the bay, and the winds got too high, I could be driven aground. Besides that, it would be dangerous to try to clean a hull with much chop. I said, "Ah, man. A whole day of work, lost." Sid, shrugged, "Well, Jamie, that's life on the water."

I found a shady spot under a tree where the pelicans wouldn't bother me and cleaned my fish. After the job was done, I tossed the entrails into the water under a small mangrove for the crabs to enjoy, and took the hogfish into the clubhouse where I could put it on ice. No one was tending the bar when I entered. I called into the kitchen, "Stacy, can I get a Coke?" Stacy called back, "I'm going to be a minute! Help yourself." There was a sign on the bar that said that no one under 21 was allowed behind it. There was nobody around, so I went behind the bar and filled a cup with ice and soda, and then walked across the room to check out the bookshelf. The bookshelf at the sailing club is amazing. Sailors donate their old sailing books to the club. You can read them there for free, or take them home if you donate a couple of bucks to their charity fund.

I was thumbing through a 1970s cruising guide for the Bahamas when Stacy came out of the kitchen and said, "Oh! Jamie, it's you. Hey, um...the Sheriff's Department called about you." I said, "What? Why would they call here about me?" She said, "They didn't call about you, exactly. They didn't give me the details, but they said that something happened with your mom, and that they would send someone to come pick you up." I was confused and worried. "That's all they said? Was she in an accident? Did they say if she was alright?" Stacy said, "Jamie, I don't know. I'm sure that everything's going to be okay."

I walked outside and checked my phone for messages. There weren't any. I called Mom's cell, but it went to voicemail, "Hello. This is Rosa Bonifacio. I'm sorry that I missed you. Please leave a message and I will return your call as soon as possible. Thank you." I felt a little sick when it occurred to me that that might be the last time I would ever hear my mother's voice. Had she been in a car accident? That made the most sense. It's like paradise here, but everyone is angry, especially when they're driving. I wondered if I'd been orphaned by some retiree with road rage. I often think that the drivers here weren't paying attention in physics class when the teacher said that no two particles of matter can occupy the same space at the same time. I realized that I was pacing up and down the dock, so I went aboard Eagle Ray, stowed the weatherboards, and went into the cabin and tried to wait patiently. Unfortunately, patience has never been one of my virtues. I went outside and began pacing up and down the dock again. Then, it occurred to me that the police wouldn't have known how to find me if Mom hadn't told them. At least I knew that she was alive.

An hour later, a white SUV with a Florida Department of Human Services logo parked in front of the clubhouse. I ran to the parking lot and a middle-aged woman in a pantsuit got out of the vehicle. She said, "Are you Jaime Bonifacio?" I said, "That's me. What happened to my mom?" She said, "You're mother is safe. I'm Beatrice Ridge, a social worker with DHS." She handed me her business card and then she asked me for identification. I felt relief and gratitude as I showed her my driver's license. She said, "Honey, we need to go back to my office and talk." She directed me to the passenger side of the SUV, and I got in. We took a right turn out of the sailing club boatyard and headed north, past Mote Marine Institute and the Old Salty Dog Bar-n-Grill. She turned left and headed toward Saint Armand's Circle. There's a busy round-about there, so I let her concentrate on the traffic and the pedestrians. I waited until we were on the Ringling Causeway before asking any questions.

Every time that I pass over the Ringling Causeway, I shake my head. Sarasota Bay must have been beautiful at one time. Now, it's surrounded by high-rise apartment buildings and business towers. The buildings are opulent, but I wondered how many miles of mangroves were destroyed when they developed the waterfront. Mangroves are where juvenile fish grow big enough to make it in open water. My mind was wandering off on its own again, so I yanked its leash and made it come to heel.

I said, "Mrs. Ridge, please tell me what's going on." She took a deep breath and said, "It's Miss Ridge, actually, but you can call me Beatrice. Honey, your mother's been arrested for theft and possession of controlled substances. She stole some prescription medications from one of her patients." I said, "No, that doesn't make sense. That's not something that she would do. Mom doesn't take drugs." Beatrice said, "I'm sorry, Jaime, but they have her on video. Her patient's daughter suspected that she was taking his medications and set up a nanny-cam. She reported her to the Sheriff's and they arrested her this morning." I said, "Somebody's made a mistake." Beatrice said, "You may not believe this now, but everything is going to be okay." I wanted to

21

say, "Yes, I know that because I'm the one who makes everything okay for other people. That's what I do, lady, every day." But, I didn't say that. I didn't know what to say, so I said, "Please call me Jamie. Only Mom calls me Jaime."

She drove to the DHS building near downtown and we took an elevator to her office where she laid it all out for me. She consulted a government manual encased in a white three-ring binder for a moment, and then said officiously, "On account of your mother's arrest was involving narcotics, Florida Department of Health and Human Services regulations require that you remain outside of your sole parent's custody until such time as the state deems it safe for you to be returned to your sole parent's custody." I didn't like the sound of that, and not just because of the tortured grammar. She said, "I talked with your mother. She tells me that you have no family in Florida. So, what's going to happen is that you will stay with us in our children's home for a while until we can place you with a foster family."

I said, "No. I don't think so. I'm not a child, so I'm not going to a children's home. I have school friends in foster homes and I know what that's about and I am not doing that either." She looked bored, as though she'd had this same conversation thousands of times. She said, "So, what do you think is going to happen?" I said, "What's going to happen is this; I'm going to talk to my mom and then I'm going to go home." She said, "You're a minor. It would be negligent of the state to let you stay alone." Beatrice's office felt like a jail cell. There were no family photos, children's drawings, humorous calendars, or any of the things that people put up to make an office seem less like an office. The walls were concrete and the light in the office was dim. The windows faced west, but closed vinyl window shades blocked out what was surely a beautiful view of the Gulf of Mexico. I noticed that there was a reddish-orange glow seeping into the room, between the blades of the closed window shades. It was much too early for sunset, which meant that there was no doubt about Captain Sid's information. A big storm was coming.

The air conditioning was set to an excruciatingly cold temperature. It must have been 70 degrees or colder. I felt like I was in a meat locker and I was having trouble thinking straight. I wondered why Beatrice had decided to live in Florida. She obviously didn't like the climate or the view. In an effort to keep warm, I had folded my arms and I bent so far forward that I was almost in the fetal position when I said, "Look, I don't care about the state. I don't need you. You people have found a way to make a living by pretending to solve other people's problems. Maybe you do some good for others, but I don't need your help. I already take care of everything at home. I make sure that there's food in the fridge, and that the bills are paid. You guys believe that people somehow magically become responsible adults on their eighteenth birthday, just because the law says so. But the truth is, some people are born responsible adults, and others never get there. I'm one of those people who were born responsible. I'm going to turn seventeen on Wednesday of next week. So, yeah, I am a minor. But, even so, I'm a responsible adult already. I make my own..." I swallowed hard and stopped myself short.

I put my hand over my mouth and coughed to cover for my mistake. I'd gotten carried away and I almost said that I make my own money. That would have been a huge mistake. I don't need the government involved in my business. Beatrice crossed her arms and placed them on the desk, then leaned forward and said,

"You make your own what?" I reminded myself that this person, however well-intentioned and kind, was not my friend. I said, "I make my own everything. I make my own bed. I make my own breakfast, lunch and dinner. I even make my own dental appointments." Beatrice said, "Well, Honey, you're going to be in the system for a little while." I asked, "How long is a little while?" She said, "If your mother gets probation with no jail time, and she goes to counseling and passes all of her drug screenings, you could theoretically be placed back in your home in ninety days." I was becoming desperate. I said, "Ninety days is my whole summer break. I can't have this." She said, "Well, Honey. This is happening whether you like it or not. It's best that you just come to peace with it." She asked if I would like to speak with my mom and I said, "Of course, I would."

I was told that visitations are usually conducted by video teleconference, but since the computers weren't working, I would have a contact visitation instead. It took a few hours to arrange the visitation. The DHS office and the county jail are located on the same block of Ringling Boulevard, so when we finally got the word that the visitation had been approved we were able to walk there in a matter of minutes. We went through the security checkpoint and were given visitor's badges. The officer working the checkpoint said, "Good luck in there, Bea." Beatrice said, "Thanks, Lucinda." Beatrice and I were directed to a room with a table and a few chairs. The table and chairs were bolted to the concrete floor. A very polite jailer entered the room with Mom and gently conducted her to a chair and then asked me to please have a seat in the chair opposite her. Beatrice and the jailer were obviously acquainted. They moved to a corner of the room and engaged in their own discussion. The effect of hearing their voices echoing off of the cinder block walls, and trying to concentrate on my own conversation was confusing and a little disorienting. It would have been less distracting if they'd been eavesdropping

Mom seemed almost manic, "Jaime, I am so sorry! I can explain! I've been stressed out at work. I just borrowed some Xanax and Percocet to help me sleep at night." I closed my eyes and tried to collect my thoughts. I heard Beatrice say to the jailer, "You haven't lived until you've tasted my Key Lime pie." The jailer said, "I appreciate the offer, but I just don't have a sweet tooth. I wish I did, though, because it sounds great." I said to my mother, "Mom, we don't need to talk about what happened. Let's just talk about what we're going to do next, and how we're going to make this work out right." Mom said, "Yeah, yeah. You're right. My lawyer already talked to the judge and because the jail is so overcrowded, I'm going to get probation and a fine, with no jail time. I'll be out of here in a few hours. This place is horrible, but I'll sleep in my own bed tonight!" Numbly, I said, "That's great, Mom." Mom spoke quickly, and about nothing of consequence, as she does when she's nervous. I started to feel very angry. My genetic mutation began to betray its presence as my skin turned a bright red. I heard Beatrice say, "Are you busy after work? We should go to the Columbia and have a pitcher of their world-famous mojitos. It'll be my treat." The jailer said, "You know, Bea, I'm just not much of a drinking man." They were startled into silence when frustration finally got the better of me.

I said, "Stop! You're the one who stole drugs. You're the one who was arrested. But, you get to go home tonight, and I'm the one who gets locked up. If I'm lucky, in the fullness of time, they'll let me out of kid-jail and put me in some stranger's house.

And they tell me that if you do everything right and keep your nose clean then maybe I can come home in August. I don't need this, Mom." She said, "I didn't steal any drugs! I secured and repurposed some unused medication. It's common practice." In my mind, I was screaming, "That's so ludicrous! If you need happy pills so bad, go see a doctor! They hand them out like candy here!" But, I didn't say that. Before he died, Dad had made me promise to always respect my mother. I'd lost control of my emotions and I felt ashamed of what I'd said. So, I took a few deep breaths and said "I love you, Mom."

The jailer took my mom back to wherever he was taking her and Beatrice directed me back through security. The security officer said, "Any luck?" Beatrice said, "No dice. I just can't get anywhere with that man. Maybe I'm being too subtle. Maybe he doesn't like me." I said, "Maybe he's a diabetic Mormon who was never told about flirting." I regretted saying that even before I'd gotten the words out. Both ladies stared daggers at me. I said, "I apologize for saying that." Beatrice said, "That's okay, Honey. You're not the first teenager I've ever met." Her implication was that I wasn't responsible for what I said, just because of my age, and that annoyed me. We left the county jail and headed east toward the DHS office.

I wasn't angry anymore. The emotion I was feeling at that moment was desperation. Every cell in my body was screaming for the sea. What I needed was my boat. My boat would get me my freedom. So, I invented a reason to be taken to it. I told a lie, "Miss Ridge, I didn't close the seacocks on my boat. I was so shaken up earlier that I totally forgot." Beatrice said, "Well, that's too bad. We've got to get you processed into the system." I said, "No. You don't understand. If I don't get them closed, my boat will sink tonight. It is going to happen." She said, "I'll let you call the boat place, and they can do it for you." I protested, "The boat's locked and I have the key. Even if I could find someone who was familiar with my make of boat and willing to do it, they'd have to break the lock, and they certainly wouldn't put a new one on. The first thing you know, some bum would come along and steal my stuff, or tear up my boat." She said, "Sorry, honey. This is non-negotiable."

I played my last card, "You care about the environment, right?" She said, "Of course! I'd do anything for the environment."

I said, "My boat has an outboard motor that's full of oil and I have four six-gallon gas tanks aboard. It could be sinking right now. If you don't let me close those seacocks, a lot of fish will die, and the beach at the sailing club is going to be covered with oil and gas." I was obscenely overstating the environmental impact of a sunken daysailer, but I was hoping that she wouldn't know that. I added, "We're talking fifteen minutes, tops. Five minutes to get to the slip, five to close the seacocks, and five to get back here. Please." I was more than a little disturbed to realize that I was starting to believe my own lies. Miraculously, she said, "Fifteen minutes. And, you don't say a word about this to anybody."

It took a few more than five minutes to get back to the sailing club. It was early evening and people were driving to St. Armand's to indulge in some upscale shopping and fine dining, so traffic was heavy. Beatrice was visibly annoyed. I feared that she would change her mind. After she parked, she gave me a hard look and said, "Make it snappy, Jamie. The rain's coming." I said, "Yes, ma'am," and then ran to my boat and removed the lock that kept the companionway cover secured to the weatherboards. I looked at the sky and found that Beatrice was right. Black storm clouds were rolling westward toward the Gulf of Mexico. I opened the companionway and tossed the weatherboards into the cabin and grabbed my rigging knife. I was burning precious minutes, but I wanted the cabin open in case I might need something from below. I didn't waste time pretending that I was closing the seacocks. I lowered the outboard into the water, and then primed and started it. I flicked open my knife and cut the mooring lines instead of casting them off.

Beatrice must have realized what I was doing, because she got out of her SUV and headed toward my slip. She walked over the sand driveway as quickly as her high-heeled shoes would allow. Her progress was slowed further when she reached the dock. The decking repeatedly caught her heels, but for some reason she didn't take off her shoes. There was desperation, but not anger in her voice as she cried, "Stop! Jamie! Stop! You're going to get yourself in big trouble." I grabbed the tiller and opened the outboard throttle, backing out of the slip. Beatrice made a show of pulling out her cell phone, holding it over her head, with the keypad facing me. Her fingers poised over the buttons, presumably for dramatic effect, and she yelled, "This is

31

your last chance! I'm calling the Sheriff's!" It occurred to me that she would likely lose her job as a result of doing me a favor. I felt bad for her, but not bad enough to let myself be processed into the system, whatever that meant. However, I did feel that I owed her some kind of explanation. I closed the throttle and stood up. Momentum was pushing Eagle Ray farther from the dock. I cupped my hands around my mouth and yelled, "Miss Ridge! I'm sorry!" I struggled to find words that could explain my betrayal of her trust. I was getting dangerously close to a sandbar, so I gave up thinking and said the first thing that came to mind, "I'm not a domesticated animal!"

I sat down and pulled the tiller close in to my stomach. At the same time, I pushed the outboard throttle handle hard away from me. Eagle Ray's bow turned to port, and her stern to starboard. Rotating on her center of gravity, she performed a pirouette that a ballerina might envy. After spinning 180 degrees, I opened the throttle and headed west toward the New Pass draw bridge. During the drive from the DHS office to the sailing club, I'd determined that I had one shot at escape. I needed to get into the Gulf of Mexico. I was ten miles from Big Sarasota Pass, the only

32

really safe inlet to the bay for a boat with any draft. My sailboat has a six horsepower engine. There was no way that I could get all the way down to Big Sarasota Pass and out into the Gulf before either the Sheriff's Department or the Sarasota Police Department caught me. My only chance was New Pass which was only a few hundred yards away.

There were two problems with the New Pass bridge. First, my boat's mast is thirty-one feet and four inches tall. The clearance for the New Pass Bridge is twenty-three feet when it's closed. Second, the bridge operator goes home at 6:00 P.M. They will come open the bridge after that, but it requires a three hour notice. If I'd waited three hours, then the police would have had plenty of time to come get me. I didn't have a radio, so I used my phone to call the bridge operator and request that he open it. It was ten minutes to six when I reached the bridge. By that time, the leading edge of the storm had reached Sarasota Bay. It was getting dark, and I was being pelted by cold, hard raindrops. Luckily, either Beatrice hadn't yet contacted the Sheriff's Department or she had and they were slow in getting the word out. The bridge operator flashed the traffic warning lights and lowered the barricades. Then, painfully slowly, the single arm of the bridge opened. I motored through the open drawbridge at the recommended speed.

I'd cleared the first hurdle, but that didn't boost my confidence. The second hurdle would be considerably more difficult to clear. I still had to get through the pass, which is four feet deep at high tide, and the tide was going out fast. A sailboat has a deeper draft than a power boat of the same length, so they usually avoid New Pass, because it's easy to get stuck there. It's not illegal for sailboats to use the pass, but it's also not a good idea. Eagle Ray's draft is two feet, eight inches. The pass was reported to be 48 inches deep, but soundings were rarely taken. I hoped for a foot to spare, but it was only a hope. If I didn't have enough clearance, I would run aground and be nabbed by DHS with the help of Sarasota's finest. The county would slap a big orange sticker on Eagle Ray, let her languish on the sand for a week giving prospective buyers plenty of time to ogle her, and then they would tow her in and sell her at the next Sheriff's auction.

I gunned the outboard. The late-day sun lay directly along my course and it blinded me a little, so I put on my Oakleys. I looked over the gunwale, but the water was too murky to see through. Suddenly, Eagle Ray lurched to a stop and I was thrown forward through the companionway. My body struck the cabin sole hard and I reflexively said, "Bloody sand bar!" I climbed back into the cockpit and assessed the situation. The outboard had died, so I restarted it. I tried reversing the engine, and turning the tiller back and forth. I got a little movement, but not enough to pull free. The sandbars along New Pass had obviously shifted since the last time I'd made use of it. I'd guessed wrong about the location of the center of the channel and had aimed too far to starboard. I set the outboard to reverse at idle speed, and secured the tiller to a starboard cleat, which would turn the bow to port if my plan worked.

I climbed halfway up the mast and hung from the shroud spreader and then swung my legs back and forth, which made the boat rock. From my vantage point, I could see Beatrice Ridge and a deputy standing on the New Pass Bridge. It looked like he was talking into a radio, and I guessed that it wouldn't be long before a city or county patrol boat showed up. Eagle Ray groaned as she pulled off of the sandbar and began crawling backward. I tossed my length of seatbelt into the cockpit and slid down the mast. I untied the tiller, put the engine into forward and headed for the waves breaking at the mouth of the pass. I opened the throttle and pointed my bow toward the fading light of the setting sun, and away from the storm behind me.

Chapter Two

Due to the storm, darkness fell nearly as soon as I'd cleared New Pass. After half an hour, I'd covered nearly four miles. I was free, but it might be a job to stay that way. If I were a Sheriff's Deputy, I would alert the department's boat units and contact the Coast Guard. I doubted that the county would send up a helicopter just for this, especially in this weather. I hoped that they would just issue a "be on the lookout" and leave it at that. I didn't know anything about police procedure, but I thought it would be best to assume that the authorities were looking for me. A small fiberglass sailboat like mine doesn't show up well on radar. In fact, to avoid collisions with larger vessels, boats like mine usually have a radar reflector hanging in the rigging. I decided that it was worth the risk to haul the radar reflector down from the mast. I also turned off all of my running lights. It was an unsafe thing to do, especially on a dark night. The outboard didn't make a great deal of noise, but I killed it and raised my sails anyway. The wind ripped at her sails and pushed Eagle Ray across the water faster than I could ever remember sailing her. Just to be safe, I turned off my phone and removed its battery. Now, I had to decide in which direction to sail. I reasoned that if I stayed close to shore, I would inevitably be spotted by someone. It made the most sense to continue to run directly before the wind, due west, and get as far into the Gulf of Mexico as possible.

There was a slight chop, but the seas weren't high enough to limit my speed by much. In the morning, I would have to heave to and find my position. I would also have to conduct an inventory of the boat. I had exactly twenty gallons of water onboard, as well as a small solar still, so water was not an issue. I eat lunch onboard when I'm working. Since today was my first full day back at work, Eagle Ray was stocked up on food. I had enough canned goods to last a week, if not more. I also had my spear-fishing stuff, all of my freediving gear, a fishing pole and a small propane grill. I had a couple of spare shirts, some long pants and swim trunks. I wasn't sure exactly what I was trying to do, but whatever it was, it seemed very doable.

I sailed through the night. At around seven the next morning I heaved-to and furled my sails. I checked my GPS and found that I'd sailed 60 miles into the Gulf. I'd averaged 5 knots. That's pretty good, considering Eagle Ray's top speed is around 7 knots. It took me twelve hours to cover the distance that a motorboat could cover easily in two hours. I had to assume that there was at least some kind of search for me. I doubted that there would be a major effort, but the county would certainly have given my boat's description to their patrolmen, the Coast Guard, and issued a general request on VHF marine radio for boaters to keep an eye out for a 22 foot sloop. Recreational boats under 66 feet aren't required to have a radio, but if you do have one, you're legally required to monitor Channel 16 all of the time. I didn't want to have to listen to radio chatter all day, so I never bought one.

I considered that even though I'd apparently chosen the right direction in which to flee, I hadn't yet picked a destination. I'm so tied to the ocean that I don't think of it in the same way as other people. For most people, the ocean is a dangerous place. For me, the ocean is home. It doesn't matter where I go. As long as I'm on the water, I'm where I want to be. I was exhausted from sailing all night. I hugged the mast, closed my eyes, and let my mind wander for a moment. My family still owned a small house and a few acres of land on Culebra. We used to stay there when visiting family. The last time I'd been there was three years ago. I made up my mind. I would sail to Culebra. I vaguely remembered that Culebra was about 1500 miles away by air. I wasn't sure what that translated to in sea miles, but it would be quite a bit more. It didn't matter, I had made a decision. Culebra was my destination. I would get there when I got there. I felt the boat rock with the gentle swell. I felt the cool, salty breeze still blowing from the east. Standing on the deck, leaning against the mast, under the warming sun...I fell asleep and then fell onto the deck. The boat was listing to starboard, so I fell to my right and slid toward the gunwale and the Gulf of Mexico. Luckily, I came awake soon enough to raise my arms and grab the lifeline. I swung my leg around a stanchion and hauled myself back onto the deck. I said aloud, "Okay. I need some sleep." I dropped and set the anchor and then hung an edge of my sea anchor over both the port and starboard sides of the stern, so as to obscure the name of my boat. I also hauled the black anchor ball up into the rigging. Technically, a vessel under twenty-three feet is not legally required to show an anchor shape or anchor light in most locations. But, why draw attention? When I was satisfied that Eagle Ray was as secure as I could make it, I crawled into the cabin, drank a glass of water, curled up in the V-berth and fell asleep.

I woke around midday. I grabbed a can of tuna and some crackers and went up on deck. The gulf was calm and quiet, and the sun was warm. A frigate bird was gliding in large circles around Eagle Ray. It was a particularly large specimen, with a wingspan that could have been six or seven feet. Frigate birds eat the fish and squid that swim to the surface in an attempt to escape large predators. There must have been a tuna, marlin or other big fish nearby. No sooner had I made that connection than a mass of flying fish came skipping over the water, then some silver baitfish. I couldn't make out the species. I was startled and thrilled as a ten-foot long swordfish breached the surface! There was a rush of air as the big fish leapt from its natural element, and as it impacted the surface, a deafening slap. Involuntarily, words escaped my lips, "God, I love being on the water."

As I munched my canned tuna, I assessed the situation. I had enough food and fuel to go just about anywhere within a week, or possibly two of sailing. I could realistically make between four hundred and eight hundred sea miles in that time, if I didn't dawdle. I would need to resupply somewhere. Financing the journey might be an issue. You never know when a boat is going to need some unexpected maintenance, so I keep a grand stashed onboard. Also, I had the $140 that I'd earned today in my wallet. My life's savings, all earned through my nautical enterprises totaled almost $27,000. I've made much more than that over the years, but I cover a lot of household expenses. The money was buried in various locations around the backyard and squirrelled away in storage boxes in the attic. I keep it in the form of gold coins because they're more durable than paper money. I wish that I could keep my money in a bank where it could earn interest. But, I can't. If I did, then I'd have to answer questions about where the money came from, and I'd have to pay taxes, and OSHA would find out that a teenager was operating an uninsured commercial diving operation, and I'd get shut down and fined a trillion dollars, and then Mom and I would be back on public assistance, and that's just not going to happen.

I sometimes talk to myself when I'm alone. At that moment I was feeling angry, "I'm done with this place. It's just a bunch of jerks who think that kidnapping and extortion is fine as long as you've got a badge and a gun." I decided to write off the gold coins as a cost of doing business. Mom would need the money to deal with her legal problems. I powered up my cell phone and found that I had signal. I sent Mom an email that said that I was well. I told her where I keep my gold coins and how to convert them to cash and I asked her to please make use of the money if she needed it. I also told her that I was going to Culebra and that she should join me there when she could. I mentioned that I would check in with her in a couple of days. I turned off my cell phone and removed the battery once more. I didn't think that Mom would be allowed to be an LPN anymore. If I were in her shoes, I would untangle my legal problems, get some counseling, sell the house and go home to Culebra. I doubted that she would, though. For some reason, she thinks of PR as somehow "less than," which is weird. Puerto Rico is a great place. Besides all of that, in January Mom started dating Paul, an RN she works with. They'd been getting pretty serious and I hoped that he would stick with her through this.

After my lunch, I dipped the empty tuna can into the water to wash it off before tossing it into a trash bag. The can was oily and it slipped out of my hand and sank to the bottom. I don't throw garbage into the water, and retrieving it seemed like a good excuse to go for a quick dive. I donned my mask and fins and slid over the transom into the water. The water around Sarasota Bay is usually quite murky. Out here, the water is clear. The water was warm enough that I didn't need a wetsuit or weights. I relaxed for a moment, and looked around so that I could make a mental map of what lay beneath me. It's a technique that helps me avoid getting lost when I'm on the bottom. Today, I decided to start my descent with a tuck dive. I took three slow, deep breaths and then pulled my knees into my chest. Then, I joined my hands round my shins. My center of gravity shifted and my body assumed a head-down vertical orientation. I then stretched out my arms and legs with my fingers pointing toward the bottom and my fin tips pointing toward the sky. This maneuver reduced my body's resistance to the water and I slid down through the water column toward the tuna can lying on the remains of a long-dead coral reef.

At fifty feet, my mask became uncomfortable and the water pressure compressed it against my face. I exhaled a little through my nose and that relieved the mask squeeze. My eardrums were mildly painful, so I decided to equalize my ears. I hovered in the water column, but turned so that the top of my head pointed toward the surface. I pointed my chin upward so that my Eustachian tubes would open and allow air to move from the back of my throat to my inner ear. This relieved the pressure that had been exerted on my eardrum by the seawater. I continued my descent and when I reached the bottom, I retrieved the can and then slid it into a pocket of my swim trunks. I checked the depth gauge that I wear on my wrist and found that the depth was only 80 feet. The depth at this distance from shore should be around 100 feet. I must have anchored on a small seamount. I would record that in my log later. I would check to see if the seamount is recorded on navigation charts, and if not, report it to NOAA. I was thankful that this coral reef was already dead. I made a mental note to be more careful with my anchoring in the future.

I hovered a few feet over the reef looking for life. One of the tell-tale signs of a living coral reef is the presence of parrotfish. Coral is their food. They munch on it, digest the living animals, and poop out white sand beaches. Unfortunately, there weren't any parrotfish here. There were large Swiss cheese holes in the reef and tunnels throughout. A five-foot long nurse shark was resting in one of these. I resisted the urge to touch it. It wouldn't have caused the fish any harm, but I don't like to disturb the wildlife any more than necessary. I spent half an hour drifting around the expired reef. Besides the nurse shark and a few barracuda, I didn't see any other marine life until I happened upon a nest of lionfish. Lionfish are an invasive species. It's believed that they were introduced to the waters around Miami in the late 1980s or early 1990s. No one is exactly sure how it happened. Some people say that an aquarium was flooded during Hurricane Andrew and that lionfish escaped into the Atlantic. Others argue that lionfish eggs traveled from the Pacific in seawater used as ballast on ships. The cause of their arrival is probably going to remain a mystery. Over the past twenty years, lionfish have spread all across the Gulf of Mexico and the Caribbean. The problem with lionfish is that they prey on juvenile reef fish. There are coral reefs that used to teem with hundreds of different species of fish. Now, many of those reefs are devoid of much other than lionfish. It's an ecological disaster and it seems to be getting worse. Lionfish grow much larger in the Atlantic and Caribbean because the waters are significantly warmer than the waters of the Pacific Ocean. That means that they eat much more than a normal lionfish would. Lionfish have few natural predators, due to their venomous spines. If you get stuck by one of those spines, your symptoms may include intense pain, nausea, vomiting, fever, difficulty breathing, convulsions, diarrhea, and paralysis. If you're allergic to the venom, very young or very old you may also experience death.

The one good thing about lionfish is that they are delicious. In fact, they taste a good deal like hogfish. I'd completely forgotten about my hogfish from the previous day. I couldn't remember where I had left it, but I guessed that I'd left it on the bar. I hate waste and I hoped that someone cooked and ate it. I surfaced and retrieved my spearfishing gear, then swam back down to the lionfish nest. I favor a pole spear with surgical tubing for propulsion. A lot of people refer to this type of setup as a Hawaiian Sling. I positioned the surgical tubing across the back of my left hand, with one end running between my thumb and forefinger and the other running between my ring and pinky finger.

I laid the shaft of the pole spear between my forefinger and middle finger. I pulled back on the shaft and, once I had the first lionfish where I wanted him, I let the shaft shoot across my semi-closed palm. The spear entered the lionfish and I pinned him against a large piece of dead coral. Simply spearing a lionfish often will not kill it. I pulled out my trauma shears and cut the fish's spinal cord and then put it into a catch bag. I found and killed four more lionfish in the same manner. I hauled my catch onboard and gingerly removed their venomous spines with a pair of pliers and my trauma shears. Then, I cleaned them and put them in saltwater to brine until evening when I would cook them on the grill.

I was eager to get underway, but I decided to take inventory of the boat. A 22 foot sloop has a surprising number of places where one might stow a useful item and then forget about it. I found a notebook and pen and began making a list of the contents of the boat. My inventory confirmed my estimated stocks of water, food, and fuel. Sailing can get boring sometimes, so I always keep a few books onboard. I had a few paperback novels and my dictionary. I like finding new words in books. It reminds me of hunting for Easter eggs.

Even though I knew that it was there, I was pleased to see my copy of the DAN Guide to Dive Medical Frequently Asked Questions. That particular book has kept me from hurting myself on more than one occasion, especially the section on envenomation. I also found a number of things that I'd either lost or forgotten about. I found a P-38 C-Ration can opener that my Abuelo had kept from his service in the Army during the Korean War. I never met him, and I know that it sounds maudlin, but using that can opener is sort-of like my way of honoring his memory. I found a couple of spare masks and my favorite snorkel. It's a Sea Dive Twin-Blaster, and I'd thought that I'd lost it. I wished that it was yellow, but they don't make a yellow one, so mine was blue. I don't necessarily need a snorkel, but sometimes I like to float on the surface and let my body relax and breathe up before a really deep dive. A snorkel makes that more convenient and pleasant for me. I also found my binoculars and all of the safety and signaling gear that a well-stocked boat should carry, including my Olin flare gun and seven flares.

I keep a modified scuba regulator and two aluminum scuba cylinders onboard. Each of these cylinders holds 80 cubic feet of air. I obviously don't need them for diving. In fact, Dr. Carlos warned me that scuba diving would almost certainly prove fatal for me. The reason is not complicated, but it takes a little explaining. Please bear with me on this. A full cylinder is pressurized to about 3000 pounds per square inch. A person obviously can't breathe air at that pressure. It would damage the lungs. So, they use a regulator which steps down the pressure through two stages. The first stage is connected to the tank and it steps the pressure down to about 140 psi. The second stage is attached to the first stage by a high pressure hose. A diver breathes directly from the second stage which steps the pressure down to the ambient pressure of the water. A diver couldn't inflate her lungs if she was underwater and the pressure of the air supply was less than the pressure being applied to her torso by the weight of the water around her. The next time you go to a pool, take a snorkel and stand on the bottom in water deep enough for the snorkel to be just above the surface, and you'll see what I mean.

The air that you're breathing right now is around 14.7 psi. Pressure increases by 14.7 psi with every 33 feet of depth in seawater. So, a scuba diver at 33 feet is inhaling air that is pressurized to 29.4 psi. At 66 feet, the pressure is 44.1 psi, and at 99 feet it is 58.8 psi. Air is about 78% nitrogen and 21% oxygen, and 1% other stuff. When a diver is breathing air from a scuba rig at 33 feet, she is inhaling twice as many nitrogen molecules and twice as many oxygen molecules as she would inhale at the surface. I'm using the pronoun *she*, because when I visualize a scuba diver, for some reason, it's always a girl. Anyway, if she absorbs too much nitrogen and surfaces too quickly, she can experience decompression sickness, also known as the bends. If she goes too deep on air, or another breathing gas such as nitrox, she can experience oxygen toxicity. This affects the nervous system, and can cause convulsions and unconsciousness among other things, which could make a diver lose her regulator, which would lead to drowning. Oxygen becomes toxic under pressure. If a normal person breathed 100% oxygen at 20 feet or deeper, that person could die. You probably see where I'm going with this. Because my body moves oxygen through my bloodstream and tissues hyper-efficiently, Dr. Carlos estimates that if I were breathing regular air from a scuba tank, I would get an Ox-Tox hit at any depth greater than ten feet, perhaps less.

Why, you may ask, do I keep something that can kill me on my boat? I need it for buoyancy. I keep my salving equipment under the bunk in the V-berth. I have two 75 lb. lift bags that I use for raising relatively small objects, such as outboard motors and other things that like to fall overboard. I also have two sea salvage tubes which are large, sturdy air bladders that I use to raise sunken boats. It's been said that a boat's natural inclination is to sink. It's not uncommon for boats to sink in Sarasota Bay. This usually happens when a boat becomes swamped during a storm. When this happens, the owner of the sunken boat is more than happy to retain my services for the modest sum of $200. It's actually a fairly simple operation. The preferred method is to rig salvage tubes on the exterior of the vessel, but that takes a crew. I've found that working alone, it's better to fill them inside the hull. I stage the air cylinder and regulator on the deck of the sunken boat, and then lay the sea salvage tubes inside the cabin. After that, it's a simple matter of patiently adding air until the boat rises to the surface. Because I don't use scuba, I can ride the boat to the surface without worrying about getting the bends. This is useful, because I can add or vent air from the salvage tubes as needed to control the ascent rate of the boat. I modified the scuba regulator that I use by removing the primary and octopus second stages and then inserting a blower fitting into the low pressure inflator hose that would normally be used for inflating a buoyancy compensator. I found the fitting at a local dive shop. It's the same type of fitting that you might use to inflate helium balloons, and it only cost $12. I fitted the regulator with a miniature pressure gauge, known as a button SPG so that I could always be aware of my remaining air pressure. That cost about $35. I bought the regulator and the two cylinders from one of my clients for $90. The salvage tubes were free. Someone had just left them outside of Zinx's shop one day. He already had all of the salving equipment that he needed so he gave them to me. I call them my money bags, because at $200 for each boat that I've raised, they have provided a very good return on investment.

After I finished my inventory, I planned my trip. My GPS is great for navigation, but you really need a chart if you want to plan out a trip. I didn't have a chart, but I keep a road map of Florida onboard in case I want to look up the location of a town that one of my clients might mention. I pulled it out and familiarized myself with the southwest coastline. I didn't want to go too far west, because my destination lay to the east and I wanted to make good speed. However, I also wanted to avoid being identified or boarded at random by the Coast Guard or local law enforcement officers.

I decided that Key West would be my first waypoint. I had no intention of stopping there, but it provided a sort of psychological jumping off point away from the U.S. and into the Caribbean. I set Key West as a waypoint on my GPS and it gave me a heading of 135 degrees. I could have guessed that without the GPS. Due south is 180 degrees. According to the map, Key West appeared to lie halfway between due east and due south. Half of a 90 degree angle is 45. If you subtract 45 from 180, you're left with 135. It was two o'clock when I finally got underway. I started my outboard and pushed Eagle Ray forward a bit. Then, I went forward and raised and stowed the anchor. I killed the outboard and raised my sails, and took up a heading of

135 degrees. Key West lay 180 miles to the southeast. I hoped to average at least 3 knots. That would put me in Key West in 60 hours. If I averaged 5 knots, it would only take 36 hours. Of course, that's sailing time. I have to sleep sometime and I have to heave-to and anchor for that. I decided that I should plan for a week of sailing to reach Key West.

Holding onto a tiller all day can be taxing. I experimented with some lines until I'd found the right way to tie it off and stay generally on course. At midmorning a pod of dolphins came alongside and provided Eagle Ray an escort. Eagle Ray was making 3 knots. It would be fun to heave-to and go swimming with them. However, at 3 knots I couldn't afford to waste any time. In my mind, I conducted a risk versus fun analysis and decided to just go for it. I adjusted the lines holding the tiller in place until I had assumed a broad reach. It slowed the boat, but it reduced the chance of an accidental jibe. I tied one end of a 20 foot line to the aft lifeline using a simple bowline knot. I took the other end in my left hand, and using the thumb and middle finger of my right hand, I formed a double loop that I slipped around my left wrist. I think that this is called a timber hitch, but I'm probably wrong about that.

Considering what I do for a living, I should know more about knots. I fed the rope overboard, hand over hand, and then slid over the transom. I let myself sink, but held onto the line with both hands. After a moment, the line became taut and I was pulled back toward the surface. Because the boat's speed was slow, I was towed five feet under the water. The dolphins came to say hello. Dolphins are curious and they seem to enjoy interacting with people, but I doubt that they'd ever seen one trolled behind a boat before. They swam alongside me, close enough to touch. Some of them nudged me. They rocketed ahead of me and then circled back and repeated the maneuver. They raced up through the water column, breached the surface and then rocketed back down into the big blue. The matriarch of the group had at one time injured her left eyelid. A flap of scarred skin flapped up and down over her eye as she swam. It made the dolphin appear to be winking. After two of the most joyful hours of my life, the pod stopped playing. They still swam alongside me, but it seemed as though they were inspecting a curiosity. The matriarch seemed to suddenly realize that a human isn't supposed to be able to hold his breath longer than a dolphin can. In an instant, they were gone. I hauled myself back to the swim ladder, climbed aboard Eagle Ray and stowed the line. I suddenly felt very tired, so I sat down in the middle of the cockpit, Indian-style. I looked around my boat and found that everything was in order. She seemed to be making good time, listing to and fro in a contented sort of way. I wished that the dolphins had stayed around longer. Dolphins are good people.

I spent the rest of the day reading my novels and throwing flying fish overboard as I sailed. I didn't get sleepy until after ten. This time when I anchored, I took all of the appropriate anchoring precautions. I raised my radar reflector and displayed the anchor light. In 8 hours of sailing, I'd made 32 miles and finished rereading my books. According to my GPS, I was on latitude with Punta Gorda. By car, that's 30 minutes from my house. At my current rate, it would take me a very long time to reach Puerto Rico. I decided that if I passed near another sailboat, I'd ask if they had any books to trade. I didn't want to risk my location being reported to the law, but I knew that this voyage could become unpleasant if I didn't have something to read. It had been several hours since I'd eaten the lionfish and I was feeling a little peckish, so I ate a can of peaches and crawled into the V-berth. The heat of the day and the rocking motion of my boat as she swung on the anchor line sent me into a deep sleep within minutes of lying down.

Chapter Three

I made better time on my third day at sea. The wind had shifted and I had averaged 6 knots. My new heading brought me closer to the coast. I was 30 miles from shore when I anchored at sunset. My latitude was about ten miles south of Marco Island. I was making great time. Key West lay about 100 miles south-southeast of my current position. If the wind kept up, I might reach my first waypoint in 18 more hours of sailing. The day's sailing was unremarkable, except for an hour at midday when the pod of dolphins from the previous day showed up. I knew it was the same pod because I recognized the matriarch who I'd decided to name Winky. I decided that these must be off-shore dolphins, because coastal dolphins don't usually travel this far. I didn't go swimming with them, but I did heave-to and talk to them and pet them for a while. Sitting alone in Eagle Ray, I felt as though I was somehow setting a bad example for others, even though there was not a soul in sight. People shouldn't pet wild dolphins for two reasons. The first reason is that some dolphins are mean and will bite you. Lucky for me, these dolphins were all friendly. The second reason is that petting a wild dolphin can be considered a crime. Harassing a marine mammal carries a penalty of a $100,000 fine, imprisonment for up to one year, or both, under the Marine Mammal Protection Act. I laughed when it occurred to me that I should sue the Florida Department of Human Services for violating the Marine Mammal Protection Act.

I was beat by the time that I anchored, so I turned in just after sundown. I slept well until three in the morning, when something bumped my stern quarter with enough force to jar me awake. I sat bolt upright and hit my head on the cabin ceiling. I saw stars and lay back down on the V-berth mattress. I wasn't knocked unconscious, but I felt sick and angry. I felt like I needed to punch someone and vomit all at the same time. I'd hit my head before on many occasions and I knew that the feeling would pass in a moment or two. I hoped that my boat hadn't been damaged by whatever had collided with it. Boats make sounds when they aren't healthy. Waterfall whooshing sounds are the worst of them. It didn't sound like I was taking on water. I didn't hear any unhealthy boat sounds, but I did hear human voices.

"Hello? Is anybody home?" I called back, "One minute!" I heard a second voice say, "You're supposed to say ahoy, not hello." I was feeling better when I went on deck. I shined my flashlight around and saw two middle-aged men sitting in an 8-person foam life raft that they had tied to my starboard lifeline. One of the men was portly and had long graying hair that was tied up in a ponytail. The other man was skinny and bald. My boat listed to starboard and then to port as the larger man clambered over the gunwale and rolled into the cockpit. I said, "Whoa! It's customary to ask permission before boarding someone else's boat." He said, "But, you wouldn't turn us away?" I said, "I might. I don't know you from Adam." The man laughed nervously and said, "Actually, my name is Liberty. I'm Liberty Fenster." The skinny man said, "I'm Bobby Fenster, his brother. Can I get on the boat now?" I had them turn out their pockets but found no weapons, so I told Bobby that he could come aboard. Both were wearing Columbia shirts and trousers, a common choice for the discerning angler.

I asked the men, "Why were you in a life raft?" It was a clumsy question, with an obvious answer. Liberty said, "Our boat sank." He had an unusual accent that I couldn't quite place. It was not quite European, and not quite American. His brother had the clipped, almost northeastern pronunciation that's common in the cities of South Florida. I asked if there was anyone else aboard their boat when it sank and they said that there hadn't been. Liberty said, "We're from Naples. We were learning to fish when our boat sank." I asked, "What kind of boat were you in, power or sail?" Liberty looked at Bobby. Bobby said, "A Hatteras GT70." It made me sick to think of such a fine vessel sitting on the bottom of the Gulf of Mexico. A GT70 is 70 feet long with twin diesels, five staterooms and four heads. I would give my left arm for a boat like that. I asked, "Do you have any idea why she sank?" Liberty said, "No, we just started going slower and slower, and then the engine died. I looked downstairs, and it was full of water." I asked, "Did you hit something in the water?" Bobby said, "Nope." Liberty said, "Well, we did run into the dock a few times when we started out. There were some crunching sounds." I said, "You most likely damaged a through-hull fitting. That would have let water in. Did you notice the bilge pump running?" Bobby said, "I don't know. It was our first time out and I don't know that much about boats." I said, "You would have seen a lot of water shooting out of the side of the boat if the bilge pump was running.

If the through-hull fitting was below the water line, then the flooding would have eventually overcome the pump's capacity." Bobby said, "Does it really matter why the boat sank? It's done. Who cares?" I asked if they'd tried calling for help on their VHF radio. Liberty said, "Yes, but nobody answered our radio call. But, that's Bobby's area of expertise." I asked Bobby what channel the radio had been set on. Bobby said, "There's more than one?" I was dumbfounded. I asked myself how these people could afford a GT70. Whatever these guys did for a living, I wanted in.

I said, "A boat like yours is usually fitted with an EPIRB unit, but I don't see one on your raft." Liberty and Bobby asked in unison, "What's EPIRB?" I said, "You know. It's a little plastic box with an antenna sticking out of the top. They're usually either orange or white-and-yellow. They're supposed to be attached to the life rafts. When a boat sinks, it activates the EPIRB, which transmits a distress call and your GPS coordinates to a NOAA satellite. Then, NOAA calls the Coast Guard and they come pick you up." Again in unison, Liberty and Bobby asked, "Who's Noah?" It was difficult to believe that they weren't joking, but I answered anyway, "It's the National Oceanic and Atmospheric Administration." They both seemed to recognize the name and said things to the effect of "Right, sorry. It's been a long day." I asked them again about the EPIRB, but Liberty said that they hadn't been told about them, so they never bought one. That didn't sound right to me, but I let it go. I wished that they'd had an EPIRB unit, because the Coast Guard would have picked them up by now. Instead, I was now obliged to ferry these two diphthongs to shore.

I explained the situation to the two men. "I don't have a radio, so I can't call for assistance. That means that I'm going to have to take you to shore. I'm going to sleep for a couple of hours, and then head in. Hopefully, we'll make landfall sometime tomorrow afternoon. You guys are welcome to stay in the cockpit, or go forward to the bow. But, the cabin is off-limits." Even though the water was a pleasant 80 degrees, Liberty and Bobby were shivering. Their type of raft was made of foam and nylon webbing, so the men were soaked. Water steals heat from the human body 25 times faster than air. They had been in the water for a few hours, so I knew that they were cold. I didn't have any blankets, so I dug out my sea anchor and told them to huddle together underneath it until they'd warmed up.

It was obvious that Liberty was the talkative one, and Bobby was the quiet one. Liberty asked me, "Do you have any food?" I said, "Do you have any cash?" I don't know why I even asked that, because neither one of them had a wallet when I checked them for weapons. I know that it was a rude question to ask. I was just annoyed by the realization that during the time it would take to get to shore, these fellows would consume a great deal of food and water. That meant that I would have to resupply and risk being picked up by a cop. It also meant that I would have to use cash that I hadn't planned to use until I got to Culebra. If it had been daylight, my passengers would have seen my face turn a brilliant shade of scarlet.

I gave each of the men a can of tuna and some crackers. Liberty said, "Don't you have anything good to eat?" I said, "I'm sorry. This is a small boat and all I have is canned goods." Liberty said, "Well, your boat's a piece of junk." He looked dejected, but he still ate the tuna. Liberty was a piece of work. He'd just been rescued from almost certain death and he was already insulting my lady. I felt regret that I'd apologized to the man, and I decided that I wouldn't apologize to him again. After the men finished eating, I collected their trash and went below.

I replaced the weatherboards and closed the companionway cover, but I still didn't feel comfortable with strangers on my boat. I would have thought that the Fenster brothers would have been exhausted after a few hours in a life raft, but instead of sleeping they droned on incessantly. I drifted in and out of sleep all night long. It was still dark when the alarm on my watch chimed at five. The men were still talking, and their voices were so loud that they carried through the closed companionway as though it wasn't there. I heard Bobby saying, "The lack of explanation for their sudden absence completely eroded my suspension of disbelief." Bobby sounded smarter than he had before. Liberty said, "I agree. I actually stopped watching the program about that time and I'm sure that I'm not the only one who did. I felt that it had lost its sense of gravitas. The lead was a very one-dimensional character and I don't know why that wasn't obvious to the producers. That lead character was technically the star of the show, but that wasn't what the show was about. It was about the mission, you know? It was about four young people getting out there and using their energy and talent for the betterment of the community." Bobby agreed, "You could not be more right. I think that he was actually an incidental character. He fouled up throughout the investigation, and then when he did break a case it was because he literally stumbled into the perpetrator." Liberty said, "Fred and Velma were obviously the brain trust of the operation. Fred possessed a keen insight into the more base aspects of mankind, while Velma brought analytic and predictive power to the organization." Bobby mused, "I wonder if Fred and Velma ever got together? Their children would have been really smart." Liberty said, "There is no way that that happened. Fred was in love with Daphne. They shared milkshakes at the pizza parlor all of the time. Granted, they used two straws, but still, that represented real intimacy back then." I knew what the brothers were doing. Some of my friends have siblings who they don't have much in common with, but they still have to socialize. So, they invent games and inside-jokes to make it easier to talk to one another. They manufacture a connection that doesn't exist naturally.

Their conversation took a turn when Bobby said, "I think that Daphne is a really pretty name but that Velma is not pretty at all. But, names are just sounds. Why would I think that one's pretty and the other one isn't?" Liberty said, "Daphne was a nymph who Apollo fell in love with, but she wasn't having any of it because he was a player. So, to protect Daphne, her father Peneus turned her into a laurel tree. Apollo was still into her, so he decided that the laurel should be his official tree." Bobby asked, "Are we still talking about the cartoon, or are you doing that thing that you do?" Liberty belched loudly and then said, "I'm doing that thing." Bobby said, "Okay. I was just checking. What did Daphne's dad do for a living?" Liberty said, "Peneus? He was a river god." Bobby asked, "Was he the god of all the rivers or just one?" Liberty sounded peeved, "I don't know everything, Bobby. Why does it even matter?" Bobby sounded even more peeved, "I was just trying to be a good conversationalist and give you the stage. I don't know why anything you say matters. It's ancient history. Let it go." The bickering became louder, and I knew that I wouldn't get any more sleep, so I crawled out of my nest in the V-berth and drank some water.

68

I decided not to wait for daylight to get underway. If these guys hadn't shown up, I could have been at least halfway to Key West by nightfall, and probably farther. The sooner they were gone, the better. I turned on my flashlight and made a notation in my logbook. I'd started a record of the trip, listing May 16th as Day 1. I recorded the GPS coordinates where I'd anchored overnight and wrote, "Day 4: Rescued Liberty and Bobby Fenster. They sunk a GT70 somewhere west of Naples."

I opened the companionway cover and stowed the weatherboards and then made ready to sail. I didn't want to have to retrieve a man overboard and I didn't want my lines tangled, so I explained jibing and tacking to the Fenster brothers and what was expected of them whenever I called out, "Jibe, ho!" or "Helm's-alee!" After I'd explained the basics of sailing, I asked, "Do you have any questions?" Liberty said, "What's your name?" Out of habit, I said, "My name's Jamie." I probably should have given them a false name, but neither man asked for my last name, so I didn't offer one.

The life raft was still lashed to Eagle Ray. As simple as the life raft was, it was still an expensive one, and unfortunately too big to haul aboard my boat. I said, "We can't make any speed if we're towing your life raft." Bobby untied the line and dropped it in the water. The raft floated away. He said, "It's no big deal." As it drifted away, I thought, "Great. There's some more garbage floating around on my ocean."

Before raising anchor, I needed to make a few decisions about just where to go, so I went into the cabin and looked at my map. Marco Island is the last big town on Florida's west coast before reaching the Everglades. I was already south of Marco Island and the wind was blowing from the north. When you're tacking, it can take a long time to travel even one mile. Sailing to Marco Island was out of the question. With all of the tacking, that would take days. Even if I used my outboard, I would still be looking at a minimum ten hour trip in the wrong direction. I eliminated Marco Island as a destination.

There is a town 10 miles south, and 20 miles east of Marco Island called Everglades City. It lay exactly on my current latitude. If I turned east and took up a beam reach, the wind would probably push us 5 or 10 miles south of there. Once I got close to land, I could drop sail and motor in. Everglades City is located inside of the Ten Thousand Islands. The approach would be very shallow and there was a definite risk of running aground on a sand bar. Based on the road map, the best looking channel seemed to approach Everglades City from the south. I estimated that it would take between six and eight hours to get there. Unless these guys were keen to check out the nightlife in Key West, hitting Everglades City was really the only option. I considered asking them if they would be willing to stay on until I reached Key West, but then I thought better of it. These guys would say no to that, obviously. It's possible that they might somehow inform the authorities of my intended destination. Besides, they were really annoying people. Picking the two men up was costing me a day of sailing, at least.

I pulled myself out of the cabin and into the cockpit and said, "Alright. If things work out, I can have you in Everglades City in eight hours or so." Liberty said, "Oh, no. We need to go to Naples." I said, "Well, if we were aboard, uh... What was your boat's name?" Liberty said, "Gontercon." I thought, "Well, that's an ugly name for a Hatteras yacht." But I said, "If we were aboard Gontercon, then you could be back in Naples in an hour or two.

But, my boat is a sailboat. It doesn't go very fast, especially against the wind. It would take days to get back to Naples." He said that he understood, but I wasn't convinced that he did. I added, "We might pass some people on a power boat on the way to Everglades City. If so we can ask those people to give you a ride to shore."

With a northerly wind, I would have to sail on a beam reach on a heading of 90 degrees to find the channel that I wanted. Eagle Ray was fitted with a Bimini, but on a beam reach, it would offer very little shade. The sun's rays reflecting off of the surface of the water can burn a person badly, especially on a boat that's as close to the water as mine is. I put on long sleeves and long pants, sailing gloves, and a hat. I retrieved two one-gallon jugs of water and used a marker to write an L on one and a B on the other. I handed one jug to each brother. I said, "This is your water. Don't be afraid to drink it, because you need to stay hydrated. However, don't take more water without my permission. Trust me. I will make sure that you have enough water."

I showed them the cooler where I kept my food supplies. I said, "When it gets very hot, people don't want to eat. You need to eat a little something every few hours, because if you don't the water that you're drinking will flush the electrolytes out of your body and that can kill you. Also, there won't be enough shade under the Bimini for all of us today, but it's going to be too hot in the cabin to stay in there for very long. So, you two need to take turns sitting in the cabin and in the cockpit. You can work out the shifts between yourselves." There isn't much room in Eagle Ray's cabin, so I thought it would be a good idea to stake out the V-berth as my own personal space. I said, "One more thing, when you're in the cabin, stay off of the triangular cushion." Bobby said, "Look, kid. We're the grown-ups here." A boat can only have one skipper, and I needed to establish that fact. I said, "I'm the legal owner and master of this vessel. In accordance with maritime law, you're required to follow my instructions. Depending on the severity of the offense, the penalty for failing to do so can be a fine of up to ten thousand dollars, and a jail sentence not to exceed one year." I didn't think that was true, but it sounded plausible. I'd borrowed the language from a sign at the bait shop that warns against feeding pelicans, but I bumped up the fine and jail term. I

added, "If you can't live with that, then take the other boat."
Liberty asked, "What other boat?" I said, "Exactly."

We'd been easting in blessed silence for a couple of hours
when curiosity got the better of me. Liberty was sitting beside me
in the cockpit, so I asked, "Where did you get the name for your
boat?" Liberty said, "It's a funny story. You see, Father was a
lawyer." Bobby called out from the cabin, "Liberty. That's a
private matter." I wondered; if it's a private matter, then why did
they emblazon the name across the backside of their flashy
yacht? Asking about the name of the boat was a mistake. Liberty
was in a talking mood. He asked, "Jamie, why are you out here
on the ocean all alone?" I was surprised how quickly I came up
with, "It's a Boy Scout activity. I'm earning a merit badge for
sailing solo." Bobby shot me a dubious glance through the
companionway, but he didn't challenge me on it. I changed the
subject, "You know a lot about history, huh?" With more than a
little pride, Liberty said, "I hold a PhD in classical philology from
Humboldt and I lecture at a number of local universities." Bobby
amended his brother's statement, "He teaches part-time at a
couple of community colleges." I wasn't sure what to say, so I

asked, "Is Humboldt a good school?" Liberty was clearly offended. He said, "Marx, Engels, Dubois and Einstein were all associated with Humboldt." I asked, "Is it here in Florida?" Liberty said, "No. It's in Berlin. That's a city in Germany." I thought that must have been where Liberty picked up his weird accent, and probably his attitude as well. I was tired of being insulted, so I remained silent.

Liberty still wanted to talk. He said, "You said that you're a Boy Scout, so I assume that you're in high school. You look a bit older." I knew that wasn't a compliment, but I decided to take it as one, anyway. I spend a lot of time in the sun, and I've been told that it makes people look older than they really are. He asked, "What grade are you in?" I told him that I would be starting 11th grade in August. He asked, "Do they teach the classics at your school?" I actually like history, so I felt a little annoyed that I shared a common interest with this man who I disliked. I said, "They touch on it in world history, probably not as much as when you were a kid because so much has happened since then, and it's only one semester." He frowned, and I realized that I'd insulted the man without intending to. I almost apologized reflexively, but then I remembered what he'd said about Eagle Ray.

I searched my memory until I recalled something that I'd read a few months ago. I said, "You were talking about Apollo this morning. My school's library has a book on ancient Greece and I thought that the story of the Colossus of Rhodes was really interesting. Correct me if I'm wrong, but I think that it was a 100 foot tall bronze statue of Apollo. I think that it was built about 300 BC, and I think that it was destroyed by the Saracens around 700 AD, because representations of the human form were considered idolatrous. It's amazing that people could build something like that, so long ago. We think of ourselves as superior to previous generations, but in a lot of ways, I think that people were smarter back then."

Liberty said, "Your education is lacking on many fronts, young man. First of all, we don't use the terms BC and AD anymore. We use the terms Common Era or CE and Before the Common Era or BCE. Second, no one is certain of the height of the Colossus. Various accounts place it between 98 and 105 feet in height. Third, construction on the Colossus was finished in 280

BCE. Fourth, it was destroyed by an earthquake in 226 BCE. The person who told you that nonsense about the Colossus being destroyed by the Saracens is a racist." I said, "I just told you that I read it in a book." Liberty said, "Well, that book is out-dated and has no place in a modern and progressive school system." It occurred to me that Liberty was really good at reciting things that other people had written, but didn't seem capable of putting two and two together on his own. I didn't like being insulted on my own vessel, but I also didn't feel like arguing. I just said, "I like old history books better. They have more details."

The conversation had begun to feel like school and school was out for the summer. I called into the cabin and said, "So, Bobby, what do you do for a living?" He said, "I'm a letter carrier." I pictured in my mind someone toting around those magnetic letters that people put on their refrigerators. My silence must have conveyed my confusion because he sighed and said, "That means mailman." I thought of the lost GT70 and it was at that moment that I decided my life's ambition was to earn a PhD in classical philology and do whatever it took to get hired on by the Postal Service. I said, "It's too bad that you didn't record your position when your boat went down." Bobby tapped the side of his temple with his index finger and said, "Oh, but I did." I said, "That's great news! Boats can be recovered. Maybe I could do the job. I can recommend a good mechanic for the refit."

Bobby seemed amused that someone of my age would offer to raise a sunken boat. He considered his response for a moment. Finally he said, "No offense, but I think that I'll go with a professional salvage company." I said, "If you decide not to salvage your yacht, I'd like the opportunity to try it." Bobby said, "I'll tell you what, kid. If it turns out to be too expensive, I'll let you have the coordinates. But, not until after I've done my research. You know how it is. I tell you, and then you tell two friends, and then they tell two friends and so on and so on and before you know it we're all using the same shampoo." I didn't get the reference so I just said, "Oh, yeah, I understand. It's an expensive boat. You wouldn't want someone to claim her for salvage." I hoped that he really did remember the coordinates and that he would have the GT70 salved quickly, because a boat like that carries a lot of diesel and eventually it would leak out and kill a lot of fish.

By eight that morning, the wind had shifted and was blowing from the northeast. Worse, the wind was pushing black storm clouds that were dumping rain and producing a great deal of lightning. I would have been aware of the approaching storm if I'd had a radio, or had bothered to check the weather on my phone. Live and learn, I suppose. I knew that no matter what happened that I wouldn't drown. Even if I was adrift without a boat, I could probably survive on raw fish without succumbing to starvation or dehydration. However, as the skipper, I was responsible for the safety of my passengers. If we sank, the two men would almost certainly drown. I heaved-to and checked my position. There was no way that I could reach the Ten Thousand Islands before the weather hit. I could turn downwind and try to make landfall in the Everglades. I'd never sailed in bad weather before, and the kind that was heading my way looked pretty bad. If I were a better sailor, I might have attempted to make it to shore, but I was completely intimidated. At my skill level, the safest course of action was to trust the boat's designer and ride it out.

I called the Fensters out on deck and said, "There's a massive storm coming and we're going to have to ride it out."

Bobby seemed resigned to the situation, but Liberty said, "No, that's dumb. We have to go to shore." I said, "It's important that you understand that this boat does not have enough power to get us to shore fast enough to avoid the storm. We have to make the boat ready, and then just ride it out." I remembered Miss Ridge's words and parroted them, "This is happening whether you like it or not. It's best that you just come to peace with it." They grumbled but followed my instructions.

Modern sailboats are designed to right themselves if they capsize and I had faith in my Catalina. But, on the chance that the boat did capsize, I didn't want the sail or its rigging to impede the boat in righting itself. I furled the jib and lowered the mainsail. Then, I went aloft and unrigged the halyard and the boom topping lift and then went back down on deck and had the Fensters assist me in removing the mainsail and stowing it in the cabin. I made taut the mainsheet and the boom vang so that the boom couldn't swing. To avoid damage to the outboard, I drained the fuel from its lines and then moved it into the cabin. I knew that my fuel tanks were strapped down tightly, but I checked them anyway. I grabbed the tiller and unfurled the jib. It caught the wind, and I pointed my boat to the south and hoped to end up in the Florida Keys. Sailing with only the jib was wasted effort, but it was better than just waiting for the storm to hit.

When the storm finally reached us, I furled the jib and secured the jib sheets. I went below with the Fensters and replaced the weatherboards and closed the companionway cover. I found my log and made a notation under Day 4, "10:32 A.M. A massive storm arrived." What with the mainsail, outboard and Fensters, the cabin had become a tight space. I offered the Fensters the use of my humble library and crawled forward and sat down in the V-berth. The two men were looking at me, presumably for guidance. I knew that I should say something reassuring, so I said, "It's possible that we could capsize, but it's unlikely. If we do capsize, this boat is designed to flip over and right itself." I pointed my finger and made a circular motion around the cabin walls and said, "If that happens, just crawl along the bulkheads as she's rolling and try to avoid the outboard motor." Liberty said, "What if the boat doesn't right itself?" I said, "The cabin will fill with water and the boat will sink." From his expression, I thought that Liberty was going to cry. Bobby just looked annoyed. The sounds of wind and water roared outside of the boat. Eagle Ray pitched and spun, but the cabin stayed dry. The flashes of lightning through the portlights, and the bursts of thunder rattling the fiberglass hull and the smell of ozone were exhilarating. Liberty asked, "Jamie, why aren't you scared?" I said, "What makes you think that I'm not scared?" He said, "Because you're smiling. This is the first time that I've seen you smile." I just said, "A bad day of sailing is still better than a good day on land."

I slept for a few hours, but the Fensters kept talking. When I finally awoke, the storm had become violent, and I could tell that the wind was pushing us along at a fairly good pace. At this rate, I had no idea where we'd end up. I drank some water and then checked my stores. There was one cold can of chicken-noodle soup left. My food supply was gone. They had eaten it all. I ate the soup and crawled back forward into the V-berth. Liberty looked shaken, but to his credit, he was holding himself together. He said, "Jamie, you should take advantage of the time we're sharing. Since I'm here, I can give you a lecture on Greek and Roman history. It'll do you some good. Let's start with something fun. Did you know that the Sphinx is of Greek origin, not Egyptian?" I said, "Look, I'm not in the mood for trivia." Liberty brightened, "Ah! You see, there is a perfect example of how ancient history still affects our everyday lives, including our language. Trivia was another name for the Roman moon goddess Diana. She was the goddess of intersections where three roads met. Tri means three and via means way. Get it?"

I didn't have any duct tape, so I changed the subject. "So why did you name the boat Gontercon?" Bobby said, "That's private." I said, "Why can't I know? We'll probably be fish food in a couple of hours anyway." Liberty mewled. Bobby said, "Quit being a jerk, kid. We don't need that kind of talk. Can't you see he's frightened?" Liberty said, "It's okay. I'm fine. Bobby doesn't like to talk to strangers about politics, religion or money." I said that I thought that was wise. Liberty continued, "Father was a personal injury lawyer and he struck gold with a class action suit against a company that made an anti-viral drug that was used to treat chicken-pox and shingles. Women who took the drug when they were pregnant had children with birth defects. The boat

83

name is the name of the drug. It's just a little dark humor." It sounded like a sick joke to me.

I said, "I know that this really is a personal question, but if you guys are loaded then why do you have regular middle-class jobs?" Liberty said, "It's one of the rules of our trust fund. To have access to the money, we must be employed in jobs that serve the community in a practical way. Working for a charity doesn't count. Also, there's an income cap. If I made more than a hundred thousand in a given year, then I would lose access to the money the next year. You see, if we earn too much at our jobs, then we don't get the free money and that's way more than a hundred thousand per year. Bobby can't sit still, so he got a job where he could walk around all day and burn off all of that nervous energy." I had noticed that Bobby was a fidgety guy. Bobby said, "Liberty enjoys irrelevant jibber-jabber. Also, sitting is a great passion of his, so he became an academic." I had never heard of a trust fund before. The genie was out of the bottle anyway, so Bobby explained that a trust fund protects multi-generational family wealth from taxes and spendthrift descendants. I began to understand why Bobby had been so tight lipped about it. Nothing

84

good can come of being envied by others. I felt sorry for the two men. Who knows what they might have accomplished?

I was tired of talking about money. I asked, "What did the Gontercon do?" Bobby said, "About 40 knots." I said, "I meant to ask what birth defects the drug caused." Liberty said that it caused genetic mutations. That piqued my interest. "What kind of mutations?" He said, "Mostly shortened, deformed, or missing limbs, and sometimes microcephaly." I was disappointed. I'd thought I might have found a clue about the cause of my mutation and that there might be other people like me. I asked, "When did this all happen?" I assumed that the lead was a dead end when Liberty said, "Back in the 1970s." On the other hand, maybe one of my Abuelas had taken it, and the effect had skipped a generation. If they were still alive, I could have asked them. I would need to check with Dr. Carlos and see if he knew anything about that.

People can get used to almost anything, and eventually the Fensters stopped worrying about sinking and fell asleep. I enjoyed the storm and alternated between reading and sleeping. At one point, I opened my eyes and noticed that Bobby was

85

awake and that his brother was asleep. I whispered, "Are you two really brothers?" Bobby whispered back, "Same father, different mothers." I asked, "What's his deal with Humboldt?" Bobby said, "Our father was from Germany. He specialized in international law suits. He moved the family here when he found out that he could make more money practicing law from the States. He said that he chose Florida because there's no state income tax." I said, "Thank God, right?"

He looked at me with a queer expression and then said, "Yeah. Anyway, Liberty was a kid when they moved here. Father's first wife died up north on Lido Beach not long after they moved to Naples. She picked up a cone snail and it harpooned her." I said, "That's a horrible way to go. But at least it's fast." He said, "I looked up the news story when I was a kid. The article said that the poison killed her in minutes." I considered telling him that the cone snail was venomous, not poisonous, but I decided against it. Bobby continued his story, "A year later, Father married my mom, who was a paralegal in his office. It's kind of funny; one side of the family is German aristocrats, and the other side is all

Florida Crackers. I take after my mom. Liberty prefers to associate with our relatives in Berlin."

I said, "Liberty isn't a German name." Bobby laughed and Liberty snorted and jerked, but didn't wake up. In a conspiratorial tone, Bobby said, "His real name is Dieter. Kids used to pick on him in school because of his name. They'd say things like; Dieter, Dieter, booger eater. I actually came up with that one, but don't tell him. One day, he just started insisting that his name was Liberty, and it eventually caught on." I asked, "Why Liberty? Is he really into freedom?" Bobby said, "He said that he wanted a tough-guy name, so he took the name of one of Lee Marvin's characters." Dad and I used to watch old movies, so I knew who Lee Marvin was, but I hadn't seen the movie that he was referencing. I said, "He should have gone with Steel, or Finn or something macho like that." Bobby said, "He's probably better off with the name Liberty. People assume that his parents were hippies, and I think that helped him in college."

I said, "I can't tell whether you guys are friends, or not." He didn't speak for a few moments. Finally, he said, "We have to share our toys. It's a rule." I said, "I'm sorry. It's none of my business." He said, "No worries. I'm just not as sociable as he is. I've found that familiarity breeds contempt." I said, "I know that one. Machiavelli wrote that in, *The Prince*." Bobby said, "I thought that you might've read it. You seemed to be familiar with his advice that it's better to be feared than loved." I said, "Yeah, but he said that it's best to be both feared and loved." Bobby said, "Hey, we should wake up Liberty. He'd be impressed with us." I said, "Nah. Let him sleep. Poor little fella's all tuckered out."

The storm either passed us by or blew itself out by seven the next morning. I went on deck and checked my position. The wind must have shifted a number of times, because we'd been blown 63 miles to the south-southwest. Key West was just a little over 25 miles to the south. The air smelled great after the storm, so I enjoyed the morning for a few minutes and then woke the Fensters so that they could assist me with re-rigging the mainsail. The Fensters seemed ham-handed so I mounted the outboard myself. Losing the outboard would be a very bad thing. I got Eagle Ray underway and we made 5 knots for the rest of the voyage.

At half past noon we made landfall. The Fensters stretched their legs on the dock while I checked in with the Harbor Master in the marina's dayroom. They stayed close to Eagle Ray. She was a special boat, and I guessed that they appreciated that she had saved their lives. I made a notation in my log, "Day 5: I rented a slip in Stock Island Marina. The cost per foot is $3.15. The total cost was $69.30." Bobby borrowed my phone and called his wife to arrange for a ride home. Without cash, a credit card or identification, flying or renting a car was out of the question for the men. Bobby was obviously jealous of his privacy, because he walked down the dock toward the parking lot, and out of hearing range for Liberty and me. I made myself busy washing down Eagle Ray. Liberty sat on a wooden bench next to my boat. I sprayed a jet of water toward the marina's main building and said, "There's a dayroom over there where you can buy snacks and watch TV, or check your email. It's air conditioned." Liberty said, "Oh, that's okay. I'll just hang out with you. I don't mind." I said, "Do what you like. It's a free country."

I guessed that he'd been humbled by the trip, and I felt a little guilty for being so heavy handed. I didn't want to talk to the man anymore, but he just sat there watching me attend to my boat. There were several minutes of awkward silence before he asked, "Have you decided which colleges you'll apply to?" I said, "I'm not going." He seemed shocked and said, "You have to go to college. You can't be successful without a college degree." I said, "How much do you make with your PhD?" He said, "I make fifteen hundred per section and I teach three sections per semester in the spring and three in the fall and one section in the summer." I said, "That's about ten thousand a year. I make nearly twice that working part time over the summer." He said, "Well, I could make fifty or sixty thousand if I had a professorship. But, I don't want to work that much." I said, "Look, I talk to a lot of people in my line of work. And more importantly, I listen to what they have to say. So, I have a pretty good idea of how the world works, and how it's changing. When you were my age, college was cheap and it actually helped you get a job. It's not like that anymore. Unless you have a burning desire to be a doctor or lawyer or engineer or something like that, the return on investment just isn't there." He said, "Don't you care what other people think about you? How will they know that you're smart if you don't have a degree?" I said, "Aside from my family and a few close friends, I honestly do not care what other people think." The expression on his face said that he didn't believe me.

I don't know why Liberty thought that he had the right to give me advice about how to live my life, but he was like a dog with a bone. He continued to try to convince me that I should go to college. He said, "You have to go to college so that you can learn how to think right." I said, "I can think well enough already." Liberty said, "You're missing my point. You see, in my class I don't teach people what to think. I teach them how to think." I almost said a swear word. The man had been trying to tell me what to think ever since I'd fished him out of the gulf the day before.

Liberty said, "You need to learn how to make use of the dialectic." I said, "No thanks. I pee enough already." He said, "That's a diuretic. Dialectic is another word for discussion." I thought, "Well you could have just said that." He continued, "Hegel asserted quite rightly that any dialectic has three parts; thesis, antithesis and synthesis." He went on for a while about affirming hypotheses and determining confidence intervals. I wasn't really paying attention. A manatee had swum behind my boat and was lying on its back drinking the freshwater that was draining out of the cockpit through the transom. It's a crime to give freshwater to a manatee, but since it was acting on its own, I was innocent in the eyes of the law. Like most manatees, this one had scars on its body from being hit by boat props. Liberty caught my attention again when he used my name, "Jamie, people take too much on faith. Their minds are muddled by stupid television shows and religion."

I thought that Liberty's mind had been muddled by too much philology. I don't know why I felt the need to defend my beliefs to the man but I said, "I don't know a lot about religion, but I do know that God exists. About five years ago, I experienced His presence on a coral reef in the Bahamas, and that feeling has never faded." I should have just kept my mouth shut, because I'd inadvertently invited a lecture. Liberty said, "You may well have had an epiphany, or you might just be suffering from a frontal lobe disorder. Either way, my point is that your statement isn't verifiable. Any single human being on the face of the earth, at any given time throughout history could have had, or might still have an epiphany like the one you described that could reveal the existence of a God or any number of gods. However, if that did happen, then the only person who could be certain that it had happened would be the person who'd had the experience."

The conversation had become painful. I looked toward Bobby for relief, but he was still talking to his wife. Liberty said, "So, you agree that you need to go to college so that you can learn to examine the world empirically, right?" I said, "You know what? You've convinced me. I'm going to start looking at colleges and practice up for the SATs." I was lying again. I still had no intention of going to college. I prefer to just do things my own way and live with the consequences. But, I figured that agreeing with Liberty would make him happy, and maybe he would go visit with someone else for a while. I took a drink from the hose and he said, "You shouldn't drink from that. It's not sanitary." I turned off the water and stored the hose in a dockside locker. Liberty said, "Jamie, I'm glad that you've seen reason. The world is changing and you want to end up on the right side of history." I had no idea what he was talking about, and I wanted to be alone. I should have thought of it earlier, but almost as soon

93

as it came to me I said, "There's a soft serve machine in the dayroom." Liberty asked, "Vanilla or chocolate?" I said, "Both!" Without another word, he hurried up the dock toward the dayroom.

Bobby had finished his phone call and I met him halfway up the dock. I told the harbor master that the Fensters were part of Eagle Ray's crew and he allowed them the use of the dayroom. Bobby sat down on a sofa next to his brother who was busy devouring a chocolate-vanilla swirl in a cake ice cream cone. As far as I know, they spent the rest of the day watching TV while they waited for Mrs. Fenster to make the drive from Naples to Key West. I returned to my boat and donned my mask and fins. I inspected her hull below the water line and found that she was in good shape. Once I was satisfied that my boat was squared away, I crawled into the cabin and took a nap. I must have been really tired, because I slept for five hours. When the midday heat woke me up, I stretched and yawned and then went on deck. A Bentley pulled into the marina's parking lot and I said to no one in particular, "I wouldn't mind having one of those in the stables someday." I was a little surprised when Bobby Fenster got out of the car. I knew that he was loaded, but I didn't know that he was

94

that loaded. Just for fun, I visualized the Bentley painted USPS red, white, and blue, cruising through Naples with Bobby stopping every twenty feet to shove junk mail into someone's mailbox.

Bobby walked down to my slip and said, "Look, I'd like to apologize for inconveniencing you." Apparently, he'd made a trip to an ATM because he handed me $400 in twenties and said, "This is for expenses." That was an unexpected gesture, and I said, "Traditionally, sailors aren't paid for making a rescue, but I appreciate it all the same. I would also appreciate the opportunity to salve your GT70." I momentarily forgot that I was on the lam, and I handed him my business card. He took the card and shoved it into his pocket without looking at it. Then, he smiled, shook my hand and walked away toward the waiting car. Minus the cost of the slip rental, that windfall brought my working capital to $1470.70. Fortunes can change quickly on the water. Halfway to the parking lot, he turned and called out, "Good luck with that merit badge!" I called back, "Name your next boat after your wife! It's good luck!" He called back, "Bad idea! My wife's name is Mary Celeste!" I was sure that he was kidding, but I enjoyed the joke anyway.

Use of the dayroom and its facilities came with the slip rental, so I laundered my clothes and took a shower. I stepped up to a washroom sink to brush my teeth, and when I looked in the mirror I discovered that I had a beard. It was May 20th and I hadn't shaved since the 15th. I had been so preoccupied with my sailing that I hadn't noticed it growing. Now that I was aware of it, my face began to itch. I'd never grown a beard before and my first instinct was to shave it off. I weighed the pros and cons. There were several obvious advantages to having it. It made me look older than I was and obscured my features, so it was less likely that I'd be identified. Also, it might provide some protection against sunburn. Another benefit was that I wouldn't have to buy razors or shaving cream, or use my drinking water for shaving. Even though it was uncomfortable, I decided to keep it.

Chapter Four

I was still worried that I'd be found and taken back to Sarasota, but I was beginning to relax a little. Reaching my first waypoint had boosted my confidence. I was certain now that I could make this passage. If I hadn't picked up the Fensters, I would have passed by Key West without stopping. Actually, that's not quite true. If I hadn't picked up the Fensters, I wouldn't have spent any time sailing toward Everglades City, and the storm would have blown me somewhere to the west of the Keys. My guess is that I would have ended up between Key West and the Dry Tortugas. Since I had a slip for 24 hours anyway, I decided to look at the situation as an opportunity. I spent the next few hours buying supplies. Stopping meant that I could have fruit and vegetables for a day or two. Eagle Ray was much too small for a refrigerator, so I stocked up on canned goods. I've never taken vitamins, but some vague memory about sailors sucking on limes to stave off scurvy prompted me to buy a bottle. I bought a large jar of pickles. I used to get muscle cramps when working on really hot days. I heard that pickle juice can keep your muscles from cramping, and I've found it to be true. The tap water in the Keys and in a lot of coastal Florida tastes bad. I think that it has something to do with the minerals in the groundwater. So, I don't mind buying drinking water. I prefer to buy it in gallon jugs. It's more convenient, more cost effective, and better for the environment than buying smaller bottles.

After stowing my provisions onboard Eagle Ray, I stopped at a nearby boating supply store and picked up some things for the boat. I bought some extra spark plugs and plug wires, engine oil, and some zincs. I seriously considered buying a VHF marine radio. The cheapest one that I could find was $160. I decided that I would ask around the marina. Maybe someone was selling a used one for less. If not, I would come back the next day and buy one. When I got back to the marina, I lugged the two fuel tanks that needed to be refilled to the fueling area and topped them off, then carried them back to the boat and stowed them again in the cockpit lockers.

As an afterthought, I attached my scuba regulator to my air cylinders so that I could check their fill. They were both at 3000 psi. I was glad that I didn't need them to be filled. No dive shop will fill my air cylinders for me because I'm not a certified scuba diver. Because breathing compressed air can kill me, I've read a lot of manuals about scuba, dive medicine, and air cylinders. I think that counts as irony. Since I've had them, I've been a little nervous about keeping fully charged cylinders inside of my very warm boat. Long, long ago a French scientist named Amontons discovered that the pressure of a gas in a sealed container increases when the temperature gets hotter, and decreases when it gets cooler. These cylinders are hydrostatically tested every five years, with a test pressure of over 5000 psi. But still, a fully charged air cylinder is storing more than a million pounds of kinetic energy. It's highly unlikely that one of my air cylinders would explode, but if one did, it would make for a spectacularly bad day.

After I stowed the tanks and went topside, I ate a banana and thought about what I might still need to buy before shoving off. I snapped my fingers and said aloud, "Charts!" I had every chart for Florida and the Caribbean loaded on my GPS. But, I thought that it would be nice to have some big paper charts. They might not be as up to date as the NOAA charts, but I'm a tactile person, and I like paper charts. I asked around the marina. The harbor master gave me a well-used set of cruising charts for Florida and the Caribbean. He said that they had been lying around the office for years and he warned me not to trust the soundings around shallow areas. Based on the pencil marks, the previous owner of the charts had sailed from Miami to the Grenadines and back, many times over. I decided to keep the charts for good luck, but not necessarily for navigation purposes. I found a marine store and bought a copy of Waterproof Chart #16, Florida to Puerto Rico and the Mona Passage.

A little later I was sitting on my boat cleaning the winches when a girl strolling along the dock caught my attention. Actually, strolling isn't quite the right word. I'm not sure that there's a word for the way that she was walking; it was something between meandering and swaggering. Her walk said, "I don't know where I'm going, but you'd better not try to keep me from getting there." Her hair was raven black and when the sun struck it at a certain angle, it took on an almost purple sheen. She wore her hair bobbed and I thought she might have cut it herself. It was messy, but athletic and appealing. She was wearing cut-offs and a concert shirt for a band called Oleander. I hadn't heard of them.

She wore green flip-flops. They were the kind with the Brazilian flag on the plastic strap. I couldn't see her eyes because she was wearing tortoise shell Ray-Bans. Her features were fine and delicate and for some reason her nose reminded me of a painting I'd once seen of a Spanish Lady. She smiled at every single person she passed on the dock.

The girl stopped in front of my boat, gave it a quick once-over and said, "Nice knots." I felt flattered, and from the warmth in my face I knew that I was blushing a little. I said, "Thanks!" She said, "Whoever sold you the monkey that tied those knots owes you a refund." She spoke with a twang accent that I didn't quite recognize. Aside from the sarcasm, it wasn't unpleasant. I said, "There's nothing wrong with my knot-tying." That was only half true. My knots worked fine for my purposes, even if they didn't conform to generally accepted practices. The girl pointed at the stern line that I'd tied to a dock cleat and said, "Uh, huh. What do you call this mess?" I said, "I ran two half hitches around each horn. That's how I do it." She shook her head and said, "Watch and learn." She untied the line and said, "Okay. This is what sailors call a cleat hitch. Take a full turn around the base of the cleat and pass it under both horns. Wrap it up and across the top of the cleat and under the opposite horn. Bring the line back across the first wrap so that the line makes an X and then tuck the working part under itself." She gestured for me to come off the boat and then grabbed my arm and dragged me to the bow line. She said, "Now, you do it."

She was bossy, but I hadn't spoken to a girl for the better part of a week, so I wasn't inclined to object. Besides, her knot looked easier to untie than mine. I tied and retied the knot until she was satisfied that I would remember it. She stuck out her hand and said, "I'm Dara." I shook her hand and said, "I'm Jamie." Her hands weren't like the hands of other girls I'd known. They had callouses and the skin on the backs of her hands was thick and tanned. Like her accent, it was endearing. She asked, "Are you from around here?" I told her that I was from the Tampa area. She said, "Are you down here alone or with people?" I was amazed that she didn't seem to recognize my age. I was definitely keeping the beard. I said, "I'm here solo, but just to resupply and do a little routine maintenance. I'm cruising down to Puerto Rico, and I'll be shoving off tomorrow morning." She said,

"Alone?" I said, "Yeah, sure. No big deal." She looked concerned. She took a long, slow look at my boat and then said, "Permission?" I gestured her onboard. She grabbed the lifeline and a shroud and climbed over the port gunwale. She looked up at the mast and rigging, then she poked her head into the cabin and pulled it back out again. Looking stern, she stood in the middle of my cockpit, with her hands on her hips, and said, "You're kidding, right?"

She came back onto the dock and took off her sunglasses. Her eyes were electric-ice blue. I'd never seen eyes like hers before. The girl was so pretty, that it was physically painful to look at her. I didn't want to embarrass myself or her by staring, or conversely, by avoiding eye-contact. So, I used a trick that I'd learned in speech class and focused on a point on her forehead just above her eyes. She said, "Look, you can't single-hand a Catalina 22 from here to Puerto Rico. First of all, this is a daysailer, not a cruiser. Second, you can't even tie a cleat hitch. Just look at your lines. They're a mess." I don't know why, but I said, "You can come with, if you want." Again, she looked back and forth at my boat, and then put on her sunglasses. She said, "It's been nice knowing you," and then she walked away.

I borrowed a bicycle from the marina and took a ride around Key West. I rode past Ernest Hemingway's house, but I didn't go in. I probably should have, but it looked crowded and it cost money. I also passed by the Mel Fisher museum. It was also crowded, and I wanted to go in badly, but once again, it cost money, and I couldn't justify the expense. Mel Fisher was a legendary salver and one of my heroes. The man spent his entire life looking for treasure that everyone said he'd never find. When he finally found it, the government tried to take it away from him, and he ended up fighting for his rights in the Supreme Court. It was seven in the evening when I rode through Duval Street, the main drag. Key West is a little run down, and it's occupied by a diverse, noisy and colorful group of people. It's alright for a day. I'd heard that the food was very good on Duval Street, so I checked out some of the restaurants' menus. I found that the fare was much too pricey for my budget. The grouper was $30 and hogfish $50. Most places offered a tower of shellfish for anywhere from $75 to $200. I had no idea why anyone would pay that much for something that they could catch for free.

I wanted information and I knew that people are more talkative when they're sharing a meal. So, I stopped at a supermarket and bought a family size package of steaks and then rode the bike back to the marina. I fired up the grill and invited some of the cruisers berthed in the marina to help me eat the steaks. Half a dozen accepted. I cooked the steaks on my grill on the back of my boat, and we set up our cook-out on the dock next to my slip. Everyone brought something, whether it was a side dish, chips, or beverages. I really enjoyed talking to the boat people. The one down-side of hanging out with boat people is that almost all of them smoke. It's none of my business, and I certainly wouldn't criticize them for it. I think people should be free to do whatever they want to do. I knew from experience that the smell would definitely interfere with my sleep, so I decided that I would launder the clothes I was wearing and take a shower before turning in.

I enjoy being a good host and everyone seemed to be having a nice time. I like to ask open-ended questions when I'm talking to people. I almost always learn new things. People like to talk and they will usually get around to telling you something useful if you give them the opportunity. I picked up a little information, but it was mostly about weather. I asked the group at large about my primary concern, whether the Coast Guard had been boarding and inspecting boats lately. That began a discussion about a joint Coast Guard and DEA anti-smuggling operation that was currently underway. Boat people know much more than they're supposed to about that kind of thing. I think that's because so many of them are retired from the Navy and Coast Guard and still have contacts. One older man said, "Monroe County deputies have been boarding, but they usually give out warnings if you're polite."

One of the cruisers handed me a beer. Obviously, the beard was doing its job. Dr. Carlos had warned me that my mutation might magnify the effect of alcohol, and that I should avoid it. But, I was curious, so I cracked it open and took a drink anyway. It was okay, but not worth what they charge for it in stores. It was sugary but not sweet. I could smell the sugar and feel the stickiness of it on my tongue, but I couldn't taste any sweetness. The flavor of beer, if you haven't ever had one, is reminiscent of the inside of a malted milk ball, but without the chocolate. Suddenly, I felt dizzy and a little giddy, so I decided not to drink any more of it. I put the beer down and went back to my Coke. A lady cruiser, I forget her name, seemed offended and said, "What's wrong, Jamie? Not your brand? You prefer the high-dollar stuff?" I remembered the excuse that the jailer had used and said, "I'm just not much of a drinking man." The party broke up around ten and then I took a shower, did laundry and went to sleep.

At dawn, just as the sun was rising, someone knocked on the companionway cover. This time, I didn't bash my head against the cabin ceiling. Apparently, I was adapting to life at sea. I opened the companionway, removed the weatherboards and came on deck. I was expecting someone from the marina who would tell me to move to a different slip or ask me if I was staying for another day. Instead, I found Dara standing in the cockpit holding two coffees and some honeybuns. There was an Army duffle bag lying in the cockpit. Obviously, it was hers. I rubbed the sleep from my eyes, yawned and said, "Good morning,

Beautiful. Are you here to check on my knots?" I knew that she considered me a joke, so why not be bold? She handed me a coffee and a honeybun and then sat down on the portside cockpit seat. I took a seat opposite her and laid the pastry down next to me. I don't drink coffee, but just to be sociable I took a sip anyway. It wasn't bad, but it wasn't something that I'd pay money for. It did wake me up, though.

Dara stared at me for what seemed like a long time. She was still just as painfully pretty as she had been the previous day. No, that's not true. She was actually prettier in the morning light. So, again I focused on her forehead and waited for her to say something. Instead, she leaned forward and grabbed my face with both hands. I was confused and a little embarrassed, so I looked away. She said, "Look at me." I stopped averting my eyes and looked into hers. Looking into those eyes, I felt euphoric and disoriented. At that moment, those eyes were my entire universe. Green lightning bolts shot outward from deep black pupils, through electric-ice blue irises and struck at the sapphire blue coronae. Dara said, "Can I trust you?" I wanted to say anything that would make this moment last longer. I don't know where the words came from, but I told her the truth, "I don't trust anyone, and neither should you." Dara took her hands off of my face and set to work. She lowered and started the outboard. Then she untied the dock lines and shoved off. She took control of the tiller and outboard and piloted us north out of the marina. We would have to round Key West to get back into the gulf. I asked, "Dara, where are we going?" She said, "Puerto Rico, I guess."

We motored west in silence. I was confused about what was happening, and I didn't know what to do, or if I should do anything at all. After we cleared Key West Dara asked, "Do you have any spare sailing gloves and a rigging knife?" The previous evening, I'd had trouble sleeping. That was partially due to the sound of motorcycle engines and the good-time 1970s rock-and-roll that blares throughout the night in Key West. But, I'd also had trouble sleeping because I was sure that I'd forgotten to buy something but I couldn't remember what. It must have been sailing gloves. Counting the gloves that I'd been using, I had four pairs onboard, but I wear them out very quickly handling the lines. I might need a few more pairs to make the passage. My hands are calloused, but I still need gloves. If the wind caught a sail at the wrong time, a sheet going taut could still injure an unprotected palm.

I found a new pair of sailing gloves and a rigging knife in the cabin and gave them to Dara. I said, "There are only two new pairs left. Also, what are you doing on my boat?" Dara said, "I'm here to prevent your tragic death at sea." I said, "Can you expand on that?" She said, "I've been sailing all of my life and it's apparent that you haven't." I said, "I've been sailing this boat for the last three years. I know how to handle my vessel." I didn't tell her that most of that time was spent in the sheltered waters of Sarasota Bay. Dara tucked the tiller under her armpit, and then reached into her Army duffle bag and fished out a transparent dry-bag that contained a substantial number of documents and certification cards. She found her sailing log and handed it to me. According to her documents, her last name was Kemm.

Dara had sailed a lot, and her log was very detailed. I gathered from the log that she was from the southern coast of Texas. The early entries were excursions on Matagorda Bay, and around the area of LaSalle. Judging from her logs, I guessed that she was from somewhere between Houston and Corpus Christi.

That explained the accent. Later entries were more impressive. She had made several runs to the Yucatan and throughout the Caribbean. Based on the certifying signatures, I assumed that she'd made the runs with her parents. The vessels on which she'd sailed were varied.

The details in her log indicated that her parents ran a service ferrying other people's boats. It's a great niche business model. Imagine a Houston oil man who wants to take his family on a vacation tootling around the Virgin Islands, but he can't spare the time that it takes to get his yacht there. So, he hires a nice couple to sail the yacht to its destination a few weeks in advance. It's hard to get into that line of work, because you must be known to be competent and trustworthy. Building a reputation that solid takes time and hard work. Later log entries showed a couple of summers spent with Sea Trek in the British Virgin Islands, as well as time spent crewing on sailboats and dive boats for Sea Base on Islamorada.

I was extremely impressed, but I knew that no young person would rack up that much sea time without someone pushing them. It was obvious that her parents had been grooming her to take over the family business. That doesn't seem fair to me. I like cleaning hulls, but if I had kids I wouldn't insist that they do it. I'm speaking out of ignorance, but I would think that the fun in being a parent would lie in watching your children discover and realize their own dreams. I felt a twinge of guilt at that moment because I'd recalled something my dad had said to me, "Jaime, I don't care what you do for a living. I will always be proud of you as long as you are an honest man." Over the past six days, I'd told so many lies that I couldn't remember them all. If beauty is truth, and truth beauty, I was beginning to turn into a real dog. I hoped that I could make it to Culebra without lying anymore.

When I returned her log, she handed me three plastic cards that attested to her proficiency with bareboat cruising, celestial navigation, and offshore passage making. She also showed me a copy of her six-pack captain's license. I said, "Okay, I acknowledge your superior sailing expertise. That still doesn't answer my question." Dara said, "I'm taking pity on you. Be grateful." I said, "You have to give me a plausible reason for being here, or I'm taking the boat back to the marina." She said, "This little jaunt will look good on my résumé." I wasn't buying it.

After the show she'd put on the previous day, I doubted that she'd want a trip like this on her résumé. It was my turn to shoot someone a dubious glance. It wasn't lost on her. Dara knew that I didn't believe her but had chosen to let it slide.

We still hadn't raised our sails. Dara was motoring south now, into the Straits of Florida. None of this smelled right to me. I said, "So, tell me more about yourself." Dara said, "Later. Take the tiller." She killed and lifted the outboard and then raised the mainsail and unfurled the jib. She watched the telltales until they flew horizontally and then prettied the lines. It took her half the time to find the right trim that it takes me. She made an exaggerated show of pointing due south and said, "Keep her at 180 and wake me up at noon. No, make that one o'clock." Then she climbed into the cabin and laid down in the V-berth. I called into the cabin, "I don't want to go to Cuba." She thrust her head through the companionway and said, "I don't either. But, the wind is abaft the beam and I want to use it to push through the Florida Current so that we don't sail too far east. Just keep her at 180 and I'll explain it to you after I've had a chance to sleep," then she disappeared into the cabin. I checked my waterproof cruising charts. Cuba is nearly 800 miles wide, and it's the biggest island in the Caribbean. From our current position, we would make landfall there if we maintained any heading between 120 and 220 degrees. I muttered to myself, "It's my boat. I can go wherever I want." I thought long and hard about pushing the tiller over until I got a heading of 120. But, what she said made sense, so I decided to trust her.

At one, I woke Dara. She came on deck and asked for the GPS. After checking our location, she asked for the tiller and took up a heading of 90 degrees and trimmed the sails. She looked at me and said, "So, what we're going to do is sail to Great Inagua. That's the southernmost island in the Bahamas. It's about 500 nautical miles from our current location." I said, "Why Inagua?" She said, "There are two reasons. First, once we get on longitude with Andros, Inagua will block the Caribbean Current for us, so we'll make better time. The second reason is that I've never been to Inagua and I want to check it out."

Dara continued, "If the wind is still favorable, and you haven't become too annoying, I'll stay on as far as San Juan. From Great Inagua, it's a little more than 400 nautical miles to San

Juan. We'll skirt Hispaniola, but stay clear of Haiti and the Dominican Republic." That totaled more than 900 nautical miles and so far, it had taken five days to come 200 miles. At that rate, it would take at least three weeks to get to PR. Dara continued, "If the winds don't shift, it'll take us between eight and fourteen days to get there." I said, "Eight days? I'd figured that it would take double or triple the time to make the passage." Dara said, "That's the power of teamwork. We'll be sailing 24 hours a day. All vessels are required to have someone standing watch, anyway. So, we might as well spend those hours underway."

I walked forward and stood next to the mast. I was looking over the bow and enjoying the movement of the boat when Dara said, "Jamie! Let's take care of some housekeeping." I faced aft and said, "Sure. What's on your mind?" She said, "First, I'm the only person on this boat who's qualified to skipper it on this kind of trip. But, it's your boat. So, we need to address that issue." I went below and retrieved the boat's logbook. I hadn't made an entry for the day yet, so I wrote, "Day 6: May 21st: Departed Key West. I hired Dara Kemm to skipper the vessel for as long as she wants the job." I handed her the logbook and she said, "That's

115

good enough for me. There's a second issue. I'm not going to try to beat against the wind. If the wind shifts and we can't make an average speed around 50 nautical miles per day, then we fire up the outboard, put in at the nearest port, and then we'll part ways." I said, "That's perfectly reasonable." She said, "Great. Now, listen carefully to what I am about to say. I'm your skipper. I'm not now, nor will I ever be your girlfriend. Do you understand and agree?" I was offended on at least three levels. I said, "Don't worry, you're not my type." She said, "Thank God." There was an awkward silence, until finally she asked, "Just out of scientific curiosity, what's your type?" I said, "Demure." Dara suddenly noticed the relative silence around us and asked, "Why aren't you monitoring 16?" A radio! That was what I forgot to buy in Key West. I said, "I don't have one. I was going to buy one today. No worries. I'll get one in the Bahamas." She sighed and then shook her head and rolled her eyes. Dara said, "Do you at least have a passport?" I said, "I keep my passport card in my wallet, always."

Dara's housekeeping lecture gradually became a friendly conversation. She said, "I just finished my freshman year at A&M Galveston. I was studying marine biology." I noted that she'd used the past tense. I said, "That sounds like an interesting field." Dara said, "It's interesting, but I'm a little tired of school. I'm a scuba instructor. I thought that I would spend a little time crewing yachts and working the dive boats. You know, just exploring the Caribbean. Big yachts often put in at Key West so I flew down to look for a gig." I said, "And you found one!" She said, "I meant a paying gig." I said, "You're being paid in friendship, the only thing that really matters in life." Her response surprised me. Her expression was shaded by a little sadness and she said, "Too true." I suspected that Dara had left someone in Key West, but I didn't press her about it.

I asked Dara which organization she taught through and she said that she was a NAUI instructor. I had taken their skin diver course and their first aid and CPR course from a local dive shop. The training was excellent. I didn't need the skin diving course, but I was curious about how normal people go about learning to freedive. I also wanted to learn about other people's limitations, and what to do if I ever needed to help a freediver in trouble. I like to be aware of what's happening in my ocean, so I spend a lot of time talking to divers and scuba instructors. You can pick up a lot of information by just hanging out and listening.

I said, "Most of the shops in the Caribbean are PADI shops. That may be changing, though. The people at SSI are making inroads due to their aggressive pricing and the fact that their dive shops can print their own certification cards." I didn't really know what I was talking about. I was just parroting something that I'd heard before. Dara said, "I don't care about that stuff. I only teach private lessons. Besides, any operation would be happy to hire a NAUI DM to work the boats." I asked, "Why did you go with NAUI?" She said, "I like that they stress freediving skills. I want my students to be comfortable with mask, fins, and snorkel before putting them on scuba. It reduces the effect of task loading. I also think that it makes for safer scuba divers. I mean, running out of air is inexcusable. But, what if someone does? That person just became a freediver."

I asked, "Do you freedive?" She said, "I took a PFI course, but I don't do it often because I don't have any freediving buddies." Freedivers never dive without support because there's a danger of blacking out and drowning. I had known for a long time that I was probably the only person on earth who could freedive alone safely, and being reminded of that caused me to feel a twinge of loneliness. I said, "If we pass a nice reef, we should heave-to, find a nice sandy place to anchor and have a swim." Dara smiled and said, "You got that right, Brother. We could change course a bit and hit Cay Sal Bank. If we did, we could be near the Anguilla Cays this time tomorrow. Shall we put it on the itinerary?" I said, "Absolutely!" But, I was thinking, "Great! Now she thinks of me as a brother." She consulted one of her notebooks and then typed new coordinates into the GPS. She bore off of 90 degrees and took up a heading of 125.

Before the day was out, I'd come to realize what a lucky break it was that Dara had decided to hijack Eagle Ray. I had believed that I was a competent sailor until I met Dara. After a few hours with her, I knew that I wasn't even close. She was incredibly knowledgeable. She told me things about my own boat's construction and performance that weren't even in the owner's manual. She explained the physics of sailing, and taught me the technical terms for the effects that I was already familiar with. I knew that it was a good thing to have a little pressure working on the tiller, because if I had to let go of it, the boat would naturally head up into the wind and stop as the sails luffed. But, I didn't know that this situation was called weather helm. Dara explained that the opposite situation is called lee helm. She explained that the sails don't really push a boat, but pull it due to the low pressure area on the lee side of the sail. She referred to this as lift. She also explained how the rudder and keel generate lift as well as drag. I'd read about lift in some of my sailing books, but it made more sense the way she explained it.

We invested a number of hours using the GPS to calibrate the boat's compass. Dara tried to explain the process, but I had trouble following it. She set waypoints on the GPS along the 90 degree line and then sailed for two miles and checked the difference somehow and then made a slight adjustment to the compass. She said that she was correcting for half of the error. Then she turned the boat to 270 and repeated the procedure. She did this again, sailing toward 0 degrees and 180 degrees. She finally said, "It would be a good idea to check for deviation for four more compass points, but there's not a lot of ferrous metal on a boat like this and your compass was pretty accurate." I told her that I trusted her judgment, and she returned to a heading of 125 degrees. Dara spent the next few hours comparing the GPS to our charts and doing a little geometry in order to determine the Gulf Stream's set and drift. Set is another word for direction and drift refers to a current's speed. Finally, she said "Our course to steer is 129 degrees. The GPS heading was pretty close. The drift is three knots." The fastest that I can swim horizontally underwater with fins is about 1 knot. On the surface, with no fins it's really hard to make any headway at all. I suggested that we practice a few man overboard drills, and she agreed that would be a wise use of our time.

Later in the day, I found the opportunity to do a little teaching of my own. I showed Dara my salving equipment and explained its use. Dara had used lift bags before, but salvage tubes were new to her. She was very interested in learning about their operation. I felt that I'd earned some credibility when she said, "If the opportunity arises, I'd like you to show me how these things work in the water." I said, "That would be no problem if you had scuba gear." She said, "I have my gear in my duffle bag." We were both a little bored, so she dragged her gear out and we inspected it as a form of entertainment. I could tell from her kit that she was a minimalist diver. Her gear occupied very little of the space in her duffle bag. There was almost nothing to her buoyancy compensator. It was just an aluminum backplate with a small air cell and a harness. She had an Atomic regulator, and a Dive Rite octopus. Her dive computer was a clunky discontinued Tusa model made by Seiko. It was old, but she swore by its reliability.

Her pressure gauge was the same type that I use on my salvage regulators, but it was attached to the end of a high pressure hose. That was an unusual configuration. I said, "I've never seen that before. Those are completely different fittings. How did you even do that?" She said, "I hired a machine shop to make an adaptor out of stainless. It's not a big deal, the specs for the threads can be determined with calipers and a little trig." I asked, "Is it safe to attach a mini-SPG to a high pressure hose?" She said, "Why not? It's the same pressure. Maybe it's not standard, but it reduces my drag and takes up less space. What can I say? I'm an innovator."

We took turns piloting Eagle Ray in four-hour intervals. We sailed throughout the day and into the night without seeing many cruisers. However, we passed hundreds of commercial fishing boats. They were flagged by nations from all over the world. It seemed strange and a little suspicious to me that the Chinese were fishing the Caribbean. I had watch from ten to two, but Dara had asked me to wake her at one in the morning. I knocked on the companionway cover and called to her, "Dara! It's one o'clock!" A minute later she climbed out of the cabin. She checked the GPS and said, "Welcome to the Bahamas. We just reached Cay Sal Bank. If it was daylight, you would have seen the Caribbean change from dark blue to aquamarine." She snapped her fingers and said, "Just like that." I said, "I was looking at the chart. The depth changes from 2700 feet to 60 feet almost immediately." Dara said, "Yeah, and we're going to be sailing in 15 feet of water in about an hour. We need to watch out for navigation hazards now. Wake me in an hour." She crawled back into the cabin and went back to sleep.

Exactly one hour later Dara relieved me and I went to sleep. My watch chimed at six and I went topside and walked out onto the bow pulpit. The wind had freshened and we were doing 5 knots. Dad had taken us on vacations to the Bahamas a few times, but it had been several years since I'd been here and I had forgotten how clear the water is. I laid down on the deck and looked over the bow. I could see the bottom, no more than 15 feet below. We were rushing past coral heads and sea fans. I caught glimpses of reef fish, but we were moving too fast for me to make them out clearly. I turned on my side and looked at Dara. I said, "Do you feel like pulling over and taking a dip?" Dara said, "Yes, but later. We'll hit the Anguilla Cays around two."

Over the next few hours we passed at least a hundred enormous ships, with dozens of tenders buzzing off in all directions. We also passed at least a dozen Bahamian government boats moving at high speed. I said, "Don't they usually stop and clear boats like ours through customs?" Dara said, "The people in those big ships are lobster poachers from the Dominican Republic. The Bahamian authorities have their hands full with those guys right now. We'll probably end up clearing when we get to Matthew Town."

At almost exactly two o'clock, Dara heaved-to and dropped the mainsail and furled the jib. She lowered and started the outboard and said, "Here. Take this." I took control of the engine and she walked forward to the bow with her GPS and called out course corrections every minute or two. I saw something orange floating on the waves and stood up to get a better look at it. I recognized it as a mooring ball. Dara said, "Okay. Cut it." I put the transmission in neutral and Dara grabbed the mooring ball and secured Eagle Ray to it with a bow line. I cut the engine and Eagle Ray's bow turned to the south as the current caught her and the mooring line became taut.

Dara pulled our masks and fins out of a cockpit locker and handed me my gear. She scooped up seawater with her mask and laid it on the cockpit seat. She was cooling the lens so that it wouldn't fog up immediately upon entering the water. My mask had become warm in the cockpit locker, so I followed her example. She said, "It's only about fifty feet deep here. But, let's follow protocol and stick with one up, one down." Freedivers are vulnerable to a condition called shallow water blackout. They hyperventilate to increase the amount of oxygen in their bodies.

Unfortunately, that also reduces the amount of carbon dioxide in their bloodstream. An excess of carbon dioxide, not a lack of oxygen, is what causes the urge to breathe. So, sometimes their oxygen level falls too low and they become unconscious. If that happens, and there's no one to swim down and save them, they will drown. I told Dara, "No problem. Do you want to go first?" She said, "Yeah. This is one of my spots. I'll go down and check it out, and make sure it's safe."

Dara removed most of the lead from her weight belt, only retaining a little two-pounder that she positioned in the small of her back. Then, she donned her fins and mask and back-rolled over the portside gunwale. I donned my gear, and slid over the transom. Dara was floating on the surface, and I could hear her taking three long, deep breaths through her snorkel. I held onto the mooring line so that I could watch her technique without drifting. She spat out her snorkel and then executed a textbook-perfect tuck dive and slid down through the water column so silently and smoothly that she didn't disturb a single reef fish. Once she reached the bottom, Dara examined the base of the mooring line. She seemed to be satisfied that it was reliable, because she left the line and swam away to investigate a cloud of sand that was being thrown up into the air, or rather, the water by some kind of animal.

After three minutes, Dara surfaced next to me and said, "Outstanding!" She looked excited and happier than I'd ever seen her. She was breathing slowly and deliberately, to replenish the oxygen in her body. I said, "Did you see something interesting?" She took hold of the mooring line and reclined on her back, floating on the surface. Then she said, "Jamie, there is a beautiful specimen of *Coenobita brevimanus* down there that has to be at least 60 years old!" I asked, "What's that?" She said, "Oh, sorry. It's a huge hermit crab and it's living inside a conch shell. This is a very rare opportunity and you've got to go check it out. It's just about twenty feet north of the mooring line. Also, there is an octopus hole about halfway there. I made a little circle around it with shells. Octopi are usually nocturnal, but if you're lucky, you might see it come out to check out the shells." Dara's enthusiasm was intoxicating.

I pretended to breathe up, and then slid down the fifty feet of mooring line to the sandy bottom. I headed north, and sure enough, just where Dara said it would be, there was a small octopus playing with the shells around its den. When it saw me approach, it disappeared back down into its hole. I continued another ten feet, and saw the hermit crab digging furiously into the sand. That one little animal, the size of a coconut, was throwing up so much sand that my visibility was obscured for several yards to the left and right of its body, and at least ten feet up from the bottom. I assumed that the hermit crab was looking for food, and I hoped that I'd remember to ask Dara about its behavior later. The hermit crab was fun to watch, but eventually it stopped digging and settled down for a rest. I decided to swim a slow, lazy circle around the mooring line.

Dara's spot was a gem. I saw every type of reef fish that I could remember. We weren't moored near an actual reef, but rather a series of coral ledges, with several other species of coral nearby including brain coral and sea fans. I saw several species that I'd never seen before, including the stoplight parrotfish, indigo hamlet, queen triggerfish, and a single yellowtail damselfish. I saw a diamond shape in the sand, and recognized it as a stingray. Stingrays are nocturnal, and I didn't want to disturb its sleep. I changed direction, but not soon enough and it darted away. I felt a sharp tug on my left foot. At first I thought that it might be Dara trying to get my attention, but when I turned I saw that a Caribbean reef shark had bitten into my fin. It was just a little guy, about three feet long. I shoved the base of my palm into the shark's ampullae of Lorenzini, and it let go of my fin and swam away. I was wearing full-foot fins, so I was surprised that the shark hadn't pulled off my fin. But then again, it was just a smallish specimen.

I turned over on my back and lay on the bottom. The water was gin-clear and I could see Dara floating on the surface. I was feeling a deep sense of relaxation, but I could see that Dara was upset. She was waving her right hand from side to side, and when she saw that she had my attention, she pointed at her watch, pointed at me, and gave me the "thumbs up" sign that meant that I was to ascend. I swam to the surface and took a few deep breaths, pretending that I needed the air. Finally, I said, "What's going on?" Dara seemed angry. She said, "Are you insane? Or are you just stupid? You've been down for twelve minutes. You should be dead. If you want to be irresponsible and risk your life like this, then that's your business, but just leave me out of it." She swam back to Eagle Ray and grabbed the swim ladder. Then, she removed her fins and tossed them into the cockpit and then climbed onboard my boat.

I'd made a terrible mistake. I'd become so comfortable with Dara that I had forgotten to hide my mutation. Thankfully, I hadn't stayed down longer than was possible for a human. Actually, possible is not the right word. Plausible is a better one, since long breath-holds are attempted on the surface of a swimming pool, and not while freediving. I felt a great deal of anxiety as I followed Dara's lead and climbed aboard Eagle Ray. She had the portside cockpit locker open and was stowing her snorkeling gear. She held out an open hand and I handed her my mask and snorkel. I didn't want to tell her about my condition, but I felt that I owed her an apology for making her worry. After all, she was the skipper and legally, she was responsible for my safety. I said, "I should have told you that I've been freediving for a long time. I know that it's bad juju, but I usually freedive alone. I'm sorry for putting you in a difficult position. I won't do it again. I promise." Dara said, "Apology accepted." I couldn't read the look in her eyes. The hint of anger that I'd seen before was gone. She was definitely still annoyed, but there was something else. I thought that she was probably curious about the length of my breath-hold, but thankfully, she didn't ask me about it.

A couple of shark's teeth were stuck in my fin, so I pried them out with my fingers. I said, "Do you want these teeth?" Dara said, "Not really. But, hold onto them anyway. Some people like that kind of thing, especially kids." I handed my fins to Dara and she put them into the cockpit locker and secured its hatch. I said, "I wonder why that reef shark went after my fin." Dara said, "There are probably two reasons. Some research suggests that sharks like to strike things that are colored yellow. I think that it reminds them of a prey fish, like a yellow-tail snapper, or a grunt. I think it's mainly the less evolved species like reef sharks and blues that exhibit that behavior. They're not as smart as species like the great white, bulls or tigers."

I said, "Well, I like yellow and I'm not changing fins." Dara said, "I wouldn't respect you if you did." She continued, "Anyway, that leads into the second reason for the nip. A lot of dive operations stage shark feeds. I don't like it, because it alters the animal's natural behavior patterns. But, I don't have much say in the matter. The reef shark probably thought that your fin was a fish and that it was being fed." I said, "What are the odds that a shark would bite a diver?" It was a rhetorical question, and I wasn't expecting the answer that I got. Dara said, "Well, it didn't try to bite you, it tried to bite what it thought was a fish. But, for divers the probability of being bitten by a shark is 1 in 136 million. For surfers, it's more like 1 in 17 million. Surfers look just like seals from underneath."

I said, "Those numbers rolled right off of your tongue." Dara laughed and said, "The stats are from a research paper that I've been working on. I'm attempting to write something that will, hopefully, put a stop to shark culling. There are so many things in the ocean that can actually hurt or kill human beings, like the Portuguese man 'o war, lion fish, fire coral, the blue-ringed octopus...the list goes on. But, for some reason, people want to kill sharks. Last year, there were fewer than a hundred unprovoked shark bites, and only six fatalities worldwide. And even in those cases, the attack occurred because people decided to swim in a location where the sharks were feeding on their natural prey."

I said, "I didn't know that people were still culling sharks as a public safety thing. It's kind of dumb to kill off an apex predator." Dara said, "A couple of years ago, there was a shark culling in North Carolina. People just decided to go out and destroy thousands of sharks for no valid reason, and do you know what happened?" I said, "Something bad?" She said, "Yep! The sharks they killed used to eat rays. But when the shark numbers dwindled, the ray population exploded, and then they wiped out the scallops in the area. That caused the collapse of the scallop fishery. They destroyed an industry. Restoring a scallop bed is very difficult." She spent half an hour describing the process of seeding scallop larvae. It was fun to listen to her speak with such passion.

When she'd finished her lecture I said, "The law of unintended consequences strikes again." Dara said, "That's exactly right." I was enjoying the opportunity to agree with her so I asked, "Why would people do that?" She said, "Because it's fun." I remembered punching the reef shark in the snout. I don't regret doing it, obviously. I wouldn't let myself be bitten by a shark, but I have to admit that it made me feel like a big man. I said, "There must be more to it than sport." Dara said, "We anthropomorphize animals." I said, "I don't know what that means." She said, "We ascribe human characteristics to animals. We pretend that our dog or cat loves us in the same way that a human being might, but it's just not true. It's a sort of self-defense mechanism that people use to soften the harshness that comes with interacting with people. And that's all fine and dandy when you're talking about pets, but when people ascribe human emotions to wild animals, then very bad things happen to the ecosystem."

Dara went below and returned with two glasses of water. As we drank, Dara drew up a watch plan. It was very detailed, with timetables and course changes that would take us to our next waypoint, Great Inagua. Dara said, "Inagua is about 350 miles from our current location. If we can keep up 5 knots, it should take about three days to get there. For now, let's keep to four hour watches. I'll keep watch until six this evening." I said, "Actually, it's my turn. You've been manning the tiller since ten this morning." Dara said, "That's true, but I'm not tired and I really enjoy the afternoon watch." Even though she demanded it, I felt guilty that Dara was standing a double watch, until I checked my chart. A glance at the chart made it obvious that Dara wanted to ensure that we were well out of any northerly currents before she gave me the tiller again. I felt a little embarrassment that she hadn't had faith in me, but I also felt gratitude that she was with me, and keeping me and my lady on course.

Dara headed due west across the Santaren Channel. Throughout the 20 mile passage, the ocean floor lay 1500 feet below our keel. Suddenly, the depth abruptly rose to 15 feet, as we reached the giant mass of limestone that makes up the Great Bahama Bank. Dara checked the GPS and made a course correction toward the south-southeast. Dara said, "I feel more comfortable sailing in deep water. Now we have to watch more closely for navigation hazards, but at least we don't have to fight the current anymore." I took over the tiller, and Dara made us sandwiches. We ate our supper while we watched the sunset, and listened to the sounds of seabirds overhead, and the waves slapping against the hull. We didn't speak, but that didn't feel awkward. I was actually enjoying being around another person without feeling the need to keep up a conversation, and I was pretty sure that Dara felt the same way.

The rest of the night, and the whole of the next day, which was May 23rd were mostly uneventful. Dara gave me a few more pointers about sailing and navigation. Occasionally, we talked about her experiences ferrying boats, and about her college classes. We fished a little, but all we caught was barracuda. I said, "I'm kind of curious what barracuda tastes like. Supposedly, they can make you sick, but I know people who eat them." Dara said, "Dinoflagellate algae produce ciguatoxin, which gets into the food chain. Big fish contain more of the toxin than smaller fish, and barracuda are notorious for it. Ciguatera poisoning has some really nasty symptoms, like vomiting, cramps, numbness, muscle aches, and one of the weirdest symptoms, a reversal of hot and cold sensation. In my opinion, it's not worth the risk." We got tired of catching and releasing barracuda and gave up on fishing.

By six in the evening, we'd made 120 miles and we'd passed Cay Lobos. We made another 70 miles throughout the night, and at eight the next morning, we passed over Columbus Bank, the southern tip of the Great Bahama Bank. We'd reached deep water again, and were now only 100 miles from Inagua. Dara estimated that we'd make landfall around 4:00 A.M. on May 25th. The next twenty-four hours turned out to be as uneventful as the previous twenty-four had been. Just before dawn on the morning of May 25th I woke Dara for her watch. She crawled out of the cabin and stretched and yawned. Dara said, "What's our position?" I said, "I'm not exactly sure, but we must be really close. I've been smelling land for half an hour." She didn't ask me what I meant by that. She knew that when you get close to land, you pick up scents in the air, like wood smoke, car fumes, and the decayed smell of a mangrove coast.

She powered up the GPS and waited for it to register our position. Dara slowly placed the GPS on her lap and then balled her fists and began tapping them against her forehead, saying, "No, no, no. What did you do?" She showed me the GPS screen and then pointed to starboard, "We're a hundred yards from Cuba!" The GPS showed our location to be a lonely stretch of coastline near a place called Cayo Moa. I looked to the southwest, but it was still dark and I couldn't see land. I said, "I have no idea what I did." Dara said, "When was the last time that you checked the GPS?" I said, "Four hours ago at the beginning of my watch."

She examined the compass to make sure that it wasn't stuck. Then, she went below and shined the flashlight around the cabin. She came out holding a winch handle. Dara said, "Jamie, I messed up. I laid the winch handle on the bulkhead opposite the compass during my watch. I only meant to leave it there for a minute, but I totally forgot it." I said, "What's the big deal? Cuba's supposed to be our friend now." Dara said, "That's one of the problems with this situation. Cruisers aren't avoiding the island anymore." My expression must have betrayed my ignorance, so she continued, "We're at ground zero for piracy. It's like this. Imagine a reef with a few predators, but not many fish to prey on. Then one day, thousands of tasty fish show up. What happens then?" I said, "The predator population increases due to the increased availability of food." She said, "That's what's happening now. These waters are full of predators because there's so much prey." I said, "We don't have anything worth stealing, and no one's going to want my boat. It's worth two grand, tops." Dara said, "I hope that you're right, but there's a second problem. If you want to enter Cuba by boat, you have to get permission from Cuba and the U.S. months in advance. If you don't have the right paperwork, the Cubans will confiscate your boat and throw you in jail." I said, "Well, by all means, let's get out of here."

We bore away, back on a heading that would take us to Great Inagua. I said, "I'm surprised that the Cuban authorities wouldn't do more to protect their tourist trade." Dara said, "There's still a lot of animosity toward Americans. You won't hear about it on the news, but they still have American tourists locked up there as alleged spies. We've delivered boats there a few times, and let's just say that I didn't leave anything there that's worth going back for." I said, "I thought that it was supposed to be nice there." She didn't respond, but instead stood next to the mast and kept a lookout for other boats.

Fifteen minutes later, the sun had risen and Dara asked for my binoculars. I gave them to her and she asked me to take the tiller. She had spotted something that piqued her interest dead astern. She adjusted the focus wheel with her right middle finger then said, "Oh, no." I asked, "Is it the Cuban police?" She said, "No. It's Simpatico." I said, "What's Simpatico?" She said,

"That's Maldonado's cigarette boat." I asked, "Who's Maldonado?" She said, "He's a Colombian drug runner. He's part of the FARC." I asked, "What's a communist Colombian smuggler doing off the coast of Cuba?" Dara said, "It's like I told you before. He goes where the cruisers are plentiful. He put me and my folks off of boats three times. The first time was off of Bonaire, the second Dominica, and the third time near Saba." I said, "Those are all really safe places for tourists." She said, "No kidding, that's the attraction. He's after small sailboats like ours. It's perfect for smuggling. These guys will sail it to a point off the coast of Florida and then transfer cocaine from a submarine to the sailboat. They'll pay some burnout to run it aground in the Everglades. After that, it's the buyer's responsibility." I said, "Why don't they just buy used sailboats in Florida? They're cheap." She said, "Drug smugglers used to do that, but the DEA caught on. The paper trail helps the prosecutors get a conviction." I asked her how she knew so much about drug trafficking. She explained, "After the first time that we were set adrift, I boned up on the subject. Here's what's going to happen, Maldonado is going to come in fast and his guys are going to fire a few rounds into the

140

air. After that he's going to engage in friendly conversation as though we were just two cruisers comparing logs. Then he's going to put us adrift on a life raft with food, water and an EPIRB unit. He's built a reputation for sparing people who give up quietly." I asked, "So, he's a pirate who doesn't kill people?" Dara said, "Oh, he kills people, but only the people who fight back, as far as I know."

The boat began circling us. They were obviously checking us out, before closing in. Dara handed me the binos. Maldonado had good taste in boats. It was a Donzi 43 ZR. A boat like that could put out 2700 horsepower and do 100 knots easily. I didn't care for the color scheme. The top half of the hull was blue, and the bottom was painted red. In gold, the word Simpatico had been painted in large elaborate letters that ran from the bow to the stern. The font reminded me of Comic Sans. There were black crossed rifles painted inside of the O in Simpatico. I counted four men, all of them armed. They were all wearing guayabera shirts and smoking cigars.

The Donzi pulled alongside Eagle Ray and the gunmen fired into the air, just as Dara had said. They fired so many times that I wasn't sure that they had any bullets left. One of the men aboard tossed me a line but I ignored it. I wasn't going to help these people steal my boat. The line slid over the gunwale and into the water. A rotund man in his fifties with thick, silver hair gestured at the line with his cigar and said, "Mijo! That was very rude. You should always accept a line from a friendly vessel." The first man had recovered the line and tied it to an aft deck cleat, and then secured another line to a forward cleat. The silver haired man recognized Dara and said, "Dara! It's good to see you again! How are Steven and Melissa?" I recognized the names from Dara's log book. They were her parents. Dara said, "They're both well, Captain. Thank you for asking, sir." I'd not heard Dara sound obsequious before. Clearly she was frightened by this man and I didn't like that.

I would have thought that a pirate would storm any boat that he wanted to seize. This fellow was different. He liked to employ psychology. I couldn't guess how many cruisers he might have killed in his youth, before he'd gotten wise and started

142

marketing himself as the friendly pirate. Dara whispered, "That's Maldonado. Just do what he says." I whispered back, "Don't worry, I've got this." She hissed through clenched teeth, "Don't say a word. Just do what he says." Once a year, I re-read a book called *How to Win Friends and Influence People*. In the book, the author said something like, "People like people who are like themselves." I'm not sure that quote is verbatim, but it's close. I probably wouldn't be able to talk them out of stealing my boat, but it was worth a shot. I understand Spanish, but I don't speak it well. I have a particular problem recognizing euphemisms and subtext, so I try to be as direct as possible. I raised my hands in the air and said, "Amigos! No me mata! Me gusta comunistas y narcotraficantes!" Apparently, that wasn't the right thing to say, because they all looked confused and shrugged at one another. Obviously, they'd never met anyone on the high seas who approved of their chosen profession.

After a few moments of silence, Maldonado finally spoke, "You make fun. This is not a time for making fun." He switched to Spanish, "Jaime, ahora!" I was confused. I thought he was talking to me until a big man, presumably my namesake, leapt onboard and pointed a rifle at me. It looked like something out of a science fiction movie. It was plastic and curvy and the bullets were lying on top of the gun, horizontally. It was neat looking, but I didn't have time to admire it. I remembered something that my mother had told me, "It doesn't matter how big a person is; a knee is a knee. It's one of the most vulnerable parts of the human body. There are twelve muscles that support the knee, and if any one of them or a little bit of tendon, ligament or cartilage is damaged, you might never walk again." She hadn't been giving me a lesson in self-defense. She was explaining why she wouldn't let me try out for football. Luckily for me at that moment, she had allowed me to play soccer instead. I kicked out as hard as I could, and when the side of my right foot connected with Jaime's kneecap, I felt it detach from the rest of his knee. He was screaming in pain as he fell to the deck. He dropped his gun and I grabbed it.

I pressed Dara back into the cabin and turned around so that I could see through the companionway. Jaime was sitting in the cockpit, cradling his leg. His eyes were full of hatred. I pointed the gun at him and shouted, "Get off of my boat!" His friends weren't willing to risk being shot, so he had to drag himself back to the Donzi. He was swearing angrily in Spanish. I pointed the barrel of the gun at the cabin sole and tried to pull the trigger, but it wouldn't move. Dad had taken me shooting years before, but we were only using a .22 caliber rifle and a .410 single-shot shotgun. I hadn't had the opportunity to go shooting since, and I'd never handled anything like this before. I couldn't find the safety mechanism. I handed the gun to Dara and said, "You're from Texas. How do you take it off safe?" She flicked the safety off, shouldered it and fired three times through the companionway. The sound was deafening in the enclosed cabin and my ears rang and hurt. I said, "No, no! You don't understand. We're going subaquatic, Baby!" She looked confused. I said, "Give me the gun, and get your scuba gear on." It took her a moment to process what I meant by that. Her eyes went wide when she realized the audacity of the thing that I intended to do. I thought that she might protest, but she just handed over the rifle-thing and pulled out one of the Aluminum 80s. Maldonado clearly enjoyed his job because he was almost singing the words, "You're wasting your time, mis hijos! Come on out. Somebody's got to live to tell the story! It might as well be you!" Dara said, "I don't think he's telling the truth. You hurt his man, so he might kill you. He might kill me, too. I don't know." I said, "That's not going to happen."

I told Dara to cover her ears, and I did my best to cover mine by wrapping my left arm over the top of my head. My left shoulder covered my left ear and I stuck my left middle-finger into my right ear. I pointed the muzzle at the deck and pulled the trigger. A small hole appeared in the fiberglass cabin sole, but the first bullet didn't quite make it through the hull. Apparently, this gun was designed to shoot people, not boats. I pulled the trigger three more times and then the gun was empty. I heard a man say in Spanish, "Who are they shooting at? Malo, should we shoot the boat?" Maldonado shouted, "Cut the lines! Shove off! Martin, circle the boat. The rest of you, get behind the gunwale and stay ready." I don't actually know the Spanish words for shove off or gunwale, but I assumed that's what he'd said, based on context.

Seawater began to run into the cabin. Dara slid her buoyancy compensator over the top of the air cylinder and secured it with the tank bands. Dara said, "Start equalizing now, this is going to be an uncontrolled descent." We both began the exercises that would flex our eardrums and make equalization easier. She attached her regulator to the tank valve while I looked around for our masks and fins. I called out, "Where are our masks and fins?" She said, "In the port cockpit locker. They're stowed between the fuel tanks and the bulkheads." I said, "I'll get them when we touch bottom." I asked her, "Do you need lead?" She looked at the cabin ceiling. She appeared to be weighing the same question that I was. Would she benefit from wearing weight in this situation? Everything was happening fast and I knew that she wasn't sure whether she should wear weight or not. As long as she stayed in the cabin, she wasn't in danger of making an uncontrolled ascent, but there were still any number of unknown variables. Dara came to a decision and said, "Yeah. Just give me my weight belt." I handed it to her and she laid it across her lap. Her solution was a smart one. If she needed the weight, it was there. If not, she could lay it aside. I elected not to wear mine, but kept it close at hand.

The seawater was at least 80 degrees, but it felt cool compared to the more than 100 degree heat inside the cabin. The boat was almost submerged now. Seawater was rushing over the

147

gunwales and into the cabin. The sunshine through the portlights dimmed as the Caribbean Sea embraced us. Dara grabbed the GPS and said, "We need something to put this in!" We both looked around the cabin, but I couldn't find anything that would keep it dry. Dara grabbed the jar of pickles and dumped out the contents, then slid the GPS and her phone inside. I handed her my phone and she added it to the jar's contents and replaced the lid. Dara sat down on the cabin sole and looked up at the cabin ceiling and continued to equalize. Both Dara and I knew that if the boat sank quickly, either one of us might suffer a ruptured eardrum, as the pressure from the seawater exceeded the pressure in the inner ear. I noticed that she was not only equalizing in the recommend fashion, but also equalizing in reverse. While looking up and pinching her nose, half of the time she was inhaling vacuum, instead of exhaling. She was flexing her eardrum in both directions in preparation for the rapid descent.

Eagle Ray sank slowly at first. I was afraid that she might not submerge fully and instead founder just beneath the waves. If that happened, the pirates would certainly wait for us to come out of the cabin. Eagle Ray wallowed for a moment more, and then began to pick up speed as she dropped toward the seabed, stern first. I cupped my hands over my brow and exhaled a little air into the space I'd created. The airspace acted in the same way that a mask does, and I was able to see reasonably well. I could tell that Dara was having trouble equalizing and was in pain. It killed me to know that I was responsible for her pain, and that there was nothing that I could do to help.

Everything that was buoyant had floated up to the cabin ceiling. The pressure of the seawater collapsed my water jugs. The freshwater mixed with the saltwater caused the water in the cabin to take on a frosty appearance, which obscured my vision. The effect lasted only the few moments it took for my drinking water to float away. When Eagle Ray finally touched down, she didn't strike hard, but even underwater I recognized the cracking sound that must have been my rudder breaking. She sent up a plume of white sand that obscured any visibility. She listed to port which gave me hope that the keel was undamaged. I crawled out of the cabin and retrieved my mask from the port side cockpit locker. I was glad that I'd strapped down the fuel tanks. Gasoline is lighter than water. If I hadn't secured them, they would have floated away when I opened the cockpit locker. I donned the mask and cleared it with air from my lungs. After I had that on, it was easy to find the rest of our gear. I donned my fins and swam back into the cabin. Underwater, Dara wouldn't be able to see much more than blurry images, especially with the sediment floating in the water column and the lack of sunlight inside the cabin, so she had kept her eyes closed. I placed her mask into her hands and she put it on and cleared it. I pointed at her, then pointed at my ear and gave her the "Okay?" hand signal. She signaled "Okay" back to me. So far, everything was going well.

I tried to guess what Maldonado would do next. The men would be able to see Dara's air bubbles coming to the surface, but there was also air escaping Eagle Ray's nooks and crannies, and there would be for some time. I hoped that they would overlook Dara's bubbles. Maldonado might send down a diver to check for valuables. Dara offered me her octopus regulator. I shook my index finger back and forth, pointed my thumb at my chest and then gave her the "Okay" sign. She was visibly upset and tried to force the regulator into my mouth. I realized that she thought that I was going to sacrifice my life so that she could have a full tank to breathe. I found her underwater slate hanging from her BCD and unclipped it. I wrote in pencil, "Expert freediver. I'll ask for air when needed." Dara read the message but didn't believe it, and kept trying to force me to take her reg. I rubbed the old message off of the slate and wrote, "Relax. I'm fine." I checked Dara's depth gauge and it registered 62 feet. At that depth, she should have air for a minimum of 45 minutes. She could probably stay down a good deal longer. She was an accomplished diver and wouldn't be using up air swimming around.

I looked up at the surface every few minutes to see if Maldonado would send down a diver, but he didn't. The pirates just motored around in lazy circles. The boat's keel reminded me of a shark fin. The fact that they hadn't anchored was a good sign. I was a little worried that they might be waiting for one of those submarines that Dara had told me about. Throughout our wait, Dara had periodically offered me her regulator and each time I had refused it. A good deal of Dara's exhaled air was being trapped in the V-berth and it had already formed an air pocket large enough to breathe from. I considered alleviating Dara's fear for my safety by pretending to breathe the trapped air. That air wasn't pressurized to 3000 psi anymore, but it was still being acted on by the force of the water. At 62 feet, that would be about 44 psi. Dara had already depleted some of the oxygen from the air when she'd breathed it, but I wasn't sure that she'd used enough of it to protect me from oxygen toxicity. I could stick my face into the air pocket and pretend to breathe it, but if I had some involuntary reflex and inhaled, that would be it for me. It wouldn't do Dara any good to see me drown, and I wasn't sure that she could raise my boat safely. I didn't want Dara to find out that I was a freak, but it wasn't worth risking her safety just to maintain my privacy.

The sea kept us entertained while we waited for the pirates to leave. Already, various species of marine life were exploring Eagle Ray in hopes of finding shelter from larger predators. A few sergeant major fish swam into the cabin and then out again. The same happened with some small-mouth grunts and a single high-hat. I could see barracuda patrolling through the portlights. An octopus crawled into the cabin and disappeared into a cubby hole aft of the cabin. I made a mental note to look for the mollusk later. My little boat would get very stinky if I didn't find it and it died onboard. After half an hour of circling, the pirates turned Simpatico to the north and opened up her engines. They must have decided that we had drowned and written off the boat as a loss. We could hear the high pitched whine of her screws for several minutes after they'd left. Dara grabbed my arm and showed me her slate. It read, "Ascend now." I looked at her SPG, and she still had 2000 psi. I'd learned a lot about scuba from talking to divers and reading books. She had a great air consumption rate, especially considering the stressful nature of this particular dive. I wrote back, "Wait 10 minutes." I heard her growl through her regulator. She wrote, "Why?" I grabbed the slate and pencil and wrote, "It's nice down here." She shook her head, and rolled her eyes but stayed put.

What Dara didn't know was that I would never surrender my vessel, not to Sarasota County, not to pirates and not even to the sea. I knew that if someone on Simpatico was keeping watch from her stern, that they would most certainly notice Eagle Ray breaching the surface. Raising a boat, even a small one like mine is an impressive thing to behold, it makes a lot of waves and a lot of noise. From the cockpit of my boat, I can see a 30 foot mast from three miles away without binos. On a slightly taller boat like Simpatico, they should be able to see me from just a little farther. I guessed that Maldonado would order at least 30 knots and hopefully more. I hoped that if I gave them another ten minutes, then they would be at least five miles away when I raised my boat.

We'd been submerged for more than forty minutes when I wrote on her slate, "You ascend now. Stay clear. I'm raising my boat." She looked at me as though I were insane. She gave me the thumbs up "ascend" hand signal, donned her weight belt, and then swam out of the cabin. We were at 60 feet. Divers ascend at 30 feet per minute and spend three minutes at 15 feet before surfacing. That meant that I should allow her five minutes to ascend. I didn't want to wait longer than that, out of fear that she might drift away. I pulled out one of my salvage tubes and unfolded it. One was all I would need for my Catalina. Due to the construction of the boat, she would rise bow first. I didn't think that her stern had become stuck in the sand, but if it had, the tube should pull it free.

I found my modified regulator and mounted it on my second tank. A little seawater got into the first stage. It would still function well enough for now, but I was going to have to have it serviced soon or the salt would degrade the regulator's O-rings and corrode the internal metal parts. I would worry about that later. For now, I focused on feeding air into the salvage tube, a little at a time. I remembered the rudder and stopped what I was doing, and swam outside to check it. It had been smashed into a dozen pieces and wasn't worth retrieving so I returned to my task. After each time that I added air, I adjusted the tube a little to ensure that Eagle Ray would rise bow first. I didn't want the tube to escape through the companionway. After a few minutes, Eagle Ray lifted off of the sea floor and began to rise toward the surface. I vented air several times to control her ascent rate and she breached the surface more gently and quietly than I had thought was possible. In homage to Archimedes, I stood up and yelled "Eureka!" The boat was riding close to the surface, but it was high enough to allow the cockpit to drain. I couldn't see Simpatico, so I climbed the mast to take a look. From my mast, I could see six miles. I saw a few fishing vessels and a freighter, but there was no sign of Simpatico. Maldonado had obviously ordered more than 30 knots. Dara had reached the boat by the time that I climbed down from the mast. When I handed her a line, she tied it to her scuba unit and removed it. She let the unit float behind the boat and climbed the swim ladder at the transom. She sat down on the starboard cockpit seat opposite me and said, "So. One of these kids is not like the others."

Chapter Five

I told Dara about my genetic mutation, and my susceptibility to oxygen toxicity. By nature, she was a skeptic. But, since she had seen it with her own eyes, she had to believe me. Dara said, "If your doctor was right about your Erythropoietin Receptor gene having been mutated, then your ability to freedive functions in much the same way that it does in cetaceans." Dara was really smart. She knew about the gene and was able to pronounce its name. I'd had to use a pencil to scribble the name on the companionway cover because I've never been able to pronounce it correctly. Dara said, "Don't take this the wrong way, but I kind of want to dissect you now." I said, "We can probably work out a deal, just as long as you guarantee that you'll put everything back where you found it."

I was relieved to see my octopus friend crawling out of the companionway and onto the deck. I picked him up and dropped him overboard. I said, "You may have noticed my scars." She said, "I did. But, I didn't want to make you uncomfortable, so I ignored them." I described the webbing that Dr. Carlos had removed. Dara asked, "Who knows about your abilities?" I said,

"My mother, my uncle, my doctor, and now you." She said, "You should think about letting the scientific community know about this. You're obviously some kind of evolutionary throwback. Scientists could discover volumes about the development of humans from a single drop of your blood." I'd begun to feel uncomfortable with the conversation. This was an example of why I don't tell people about myself. I don't want people unraveling my DNA. That represents my life, and my life belongs to me.

I didn't tell Dara about the mess back in Sarasota. I was sure that if she knew that I was sixteen, she would turn me in to the authorities. You know, for my own good. Dara retrieved her scuba gear from the water, took it forward and secured it to the lifeline on the bow. She spoke while she worked, "Let's talk about the problem of steering without a rudder. We're going to have to steer by changing the trim on the sails. Without a rudder, the boat is going to head up into the wind frequently. That means that we're going to be working very hard. We won't be able to keep it up for long. I'm not even sure that it's worth trying."

I said, "We still have the outboard. I'm sure that water got into the engine through the air box, but I might be able to get it running." Dara asked, "How much fuel do you have onboard?" I told her that we still had close to twenty gallons. She said, "Let's see. It's about 70 nautical miles to Matthew Town on Great Inagua. Fuel consumption on an engine like this is about ten percent of the horsepower, so that's 0.6 gallons per hour. It could be more than that because she's sitting so low in the water. If you goose the engine too much you'll swamp her, but I think that she could make 3 knots in this condition. That's about six miles per gallon. So, if you can get the engine running, then we could have a range of as much as 120 miles, theoretically." I asked if there was any current to help, and she said that there was a northerly current that we would have to work against. We agreed that it would take 24 hours to motor to Great Inagua. We sat in silence for a few minutes. We were both thinking about our situation. Finally, Dara said, "If you can't get the engine running, then we might be able to attach something thin and flat to the outboard. Then, we could use that as a rudder." I told her that it was a good idea, but, that I couldn't think of anything rudder shaped on the boat. She looked up at the sky for a few seconds and then said, "We can use the aluminum backplate from my BC as a rudder." I

159

said, "That's a really good idea. I would never have thought of that. We should try it if I can't get the engine going."

I rummaged around the cabin as best I could with the salvage tube and seawater occupying most of its space. I found my tool box and removed the engine cowling and then removed the spark plug and carburetor. I used my air cylinder and regulator to blow out the carburetor and engine cylinder. I cleaned the salt off of the spark plug and the connectors of the plug wires and then poured a little gas into the cylinder before replacing them. After everything was reassembled, I attached a fuel line, set the choke and pulled the starter cord. It took a few minutes, but the engine eventually started. Dara held her breath as the engine sputtered, but when it finally ran smooth, she said, "No way! I honestly did not think that engine would ever run again." I said, "Well, you have to know how to do these things when you're a sailor."

I assembled my inflatable solar still and secured it to the bow pullet next to Dara's scuba gear. Next, I filled it with seawater and left it to do its work. The solar still is old technology but I still think that it's clever. The sun heats the water which evaporates and then condenses on the plastic housing and then runs back down into a catch basin. On a hot day like this one, the still should produce four pints of drinking water. I put up the Bimini top and we motored east toward the Bahamas. A Catalina 22 is a very dry boat, unless you sink it. Because we were riding so low in the water, waves occasionally washed over the gunwale and into the cockpit. The seas were a little higher than they had been so far, and Dara insisted on operating the outboard herself. I sat on the bow with my logbook. I thanked my past self for buying the waterproof kind. I wrote, "May 25th, Day 10 at sea. We sank Eagle Ray off the coast of Cuba, near Moa. We salved it. We intend to motor 70 miles east to Great Inagua. We expect to make landfall on the morning of the 26th." I made a mental note to do a web search for articles on effective log keeping.

Dara called over the sound of the outboard, "Jamie, I think that you should invest in a larger boat if you intend to continue making these types of passages." I called back, "If you'll skipper it, I'll buy a bigger boat." Dara changed the subject, "You know, Jamie, you could dominate competitive freediving. Once you became a name in the sport, you could make some serious money from endorsement deals." I hadn't ever thought of that, but I entertained the notion no more than a second. The consequences of following that course of action were obvious and dire. I said, "Well, that would be stealing. Freedivers dedicate years of their lives to fine-tuning their minds and bodies just to be good enough to compete in the sport. Besides that, there's a small group of people who are zealously trying to find the absolute limit to which humans can freedive. I wouldn't want to be responsible for someone's death because they were trying to dive as deep or as long as I can. Eventually, it would happen." Dara was quiet for a moment, and then she said, "This is actually a burden for you, isn't it?" I said, "Every good thing comes with a price tag."

After the escape from the smugglers I was feeling bold, so I asked, "Dara, why did you really come with me? I mean, what are you getting out of this trip? Are you running from something?" Dara ran the back of her hand across her face and sniffled. She looked around at the open sea, pursed her lips, closed her eyes and shook her head. Finally, she said, "I want to find out if I like the water." I was confused. How could anyone not like the water?

I said, "Go on." She said, "In my whole life, I've never been more than a few miles from the sea. I've never seen a mountain. I've never even seen a hill that wasn't part of an island. I've never seen snow. I don't even know how I would react to that. Beautiful little ice crystals falling from the sky? That sounds like heaven, but based on my experience alone, that doesn't even seem possible. I'm just... I feel like I'm missing something. I feel like I'm missing a lot."

Dara was an amazing sailor and I really liked the idea of her being out on my ocean. I said, "You could take your vacations in the mountains." She didn't seem to hear me. She said, "This trip is absurd. When you asked me to come with you, it was obvious that you were either joking or ignorant of what it takes to accomplish something like this. Later, when I thought about it I realized that making a passage like this one would be a good test. I'm only 19 years old. My whole life has been directed toward taking over my parents' business. When I graduated high school, I told my parents that I didn't want to ferry boats anymore and that I wanted to go to college. They were disappointed, but supportive. I'm not in love with marine biology, but I decided to major in it because that was the only field that seemed familiar to me. I was afraid to try something completely different." I was really confused so I said, "What's the bottom line?" Dara said, "I'm not some robot to be programmed by other people. I love my parents, but I just feel like I need to find my own thing." I asked, "What's your thing?" Dara said, "I don't know yet, and I may have already wasted a year of my adult life that I could have spent finding that out."

Everything that she'd said sounded like a half-truth to me. I sensed that she was nursing a wound that wouldn't heal unless it was exposed to air and sunlight. I said, "Dara, this is a safe place." That was something that a grief counselor had said to me after my father died. I continued, "It's just us two out here alone on this big blue sea. Why don't you tell me why you were really in Key West, and who you were running away from." Dara laughed and said, "Okay. I haven't been entirely truthful, and I'm sorry, alright? But I did it because I don't like talking about negative things. It brings me down. If you have to know everything, here it is. I wasn't in Key West looking to crew a yacht. I was down on a summer internship. The research vessel Havel is based in Key

West. They sail all over the Caribbean collecting fish count data. The whole thing was arranged by one of my professors."

"The day that I met you I was staying at a hotel, the Ibis something or other, just waiting for my report time. I got bored and decided to check out the boats in the marina, and that's when I showed you how to tie a proper cleat hitch." I said, "And I thank you for that." She said, "You're welcome. Anyway, later in the afternoon, I reported to the Havel and guess what? My former best friend Tiffany and her new boyfriend Vaughn were also interning on the Havel." I said, "Well that should have been a pleasant surprise." She said, "Vaughn used to be my boyfriend, but he dumped me for Tiffany. They started dating a month before Vaughn broke it off with me." The look on her face seemed to express a little pain, but mostly exasperation.

I thought that Vaughn must be a world-class idiot for breaking up with someone like Dara. My guess was that he was intimidated by her. I said, "You're a strong person. I'm surprised that you bailed on such a great opportunity just because of that." Dara said, "Jamie, you've obviously never been in love and then had your heart broken. There was no way that I was going to

165

spend an entire summer in close quarters with two people who had betrayed my trust so completely." I said, "Okay, I get that. But that leaves the question of why you hijacked my lady." Dara said, "Sometimes, you experience the fight response, and sometimes you experience the flight response. I needed to get away, and your boat was the first one leaving port." I said, "It's not just that, is it? You like Eagle Ray, don't you?" Dara said, "I liked her from the moment I saw her. But now, after all of this, I love her."

The tropical heat had become fatiguing, so for the rest of the day we manned the outboard in one hour shifts. By noon, the solar still had produced enough water for us to have a drink, and we ate a lunch of canned soup. The rest of the day was uneventful, and we didn't encounter any other boats. After sunset, the temperature dropped to a more comfortable level, and we switched to watches of four hours, so that we could get better quality sleep. Dara had just relieved me from my watch when she said, "We're in Bahamian waters now. You'd better chuck that P90 overboard." The only P90 I'd ever heard of was a workout video. I said, "Okay. What's a P90?" She said, "That's the type of gun that you took from the big guy." I crawled into the cabin as best I could and searched for the gun. It took several minutes, but I finally found it wedged between the salvage tube and the port bulkhead. I brought it into the cockpit and asked, "Is this valuable?" She said, "The semi-automatic versions sell for more than a thousand dollars. That one is fully automatic, so it would probably be worth significantly more." She seemed to read my mind because she said, "If you tried to sell it to someone on Great Inagua, you would go to prison for a long time. Bahamian law allows cruisers to have shotguns and handguns aboard their boats, but all other weapons are strictly forbidden." I asked if we should turn it in to the Bahamian police. She said, "I'd rather not have it aboard the boat when we clear customs. If they don't believe you when you tell them that you overpowered a pirate and took it from him then we're going to be in serious trouble." I said, "I don't like throwing stuff into the ocean." She said, "Neither do I, but believe me, if you have an automatic weapon on board when we go through customs, you're going to have to tell your side of the story in court." I hesitated for a moment but finally dropped the gun over the gunwale.

At midmorning on May 26th, my eleventh day at sea, we met a Bahamian Customs boat. We told them about our escape from the pirates, but in this version of the story, we shared a scuba cylinder. Our story already sounded too fantastic to be true, and I didn't want to muddy the waters. The customs officer in charge was a man named Grenville. He said, "You young people are very lucky. Maldonado is well known to us, and I've never heard of anyone who encountered him who kept his boat." I asked, "Has he been seen around here?" The officer said, "No, son. We patrol too heavily. As long as you're in Bahamian waters, you're safe from pirates." I hoped that he was right about that, and not just telling me what he thought I wanted to hear. Officer Grenville asked if I still had the gun that I'd used to sink the boat and I told him that I'd tossed it overboard. Dara said, "I insisted on that. I didn't want to risk getting in trouble for having it." Grenville said, "That's for the best. If you'd had it in your possession, I would have had to detain you until the matter could be cleared up. Do you have any other weapons on the boat?" I said, "No, the only things on board that could be used as a weapon are a flare gun, my filet knife and a couple of rigging knives." He seemed to believe us but said that he would be inspecting my boat after we got it hauled out of the water.

The customs boat towed us to Government Dock in Matthew Town. Grenville introduced us to the harbor master and explained that I needed to get my boat onto dry land so that I could repair the hull. It's handy to have a boat as ubiquitous as the Catalina 22. Charles Purvis, the harbor master, owned one and he graciously offered the use of his trailer for as long as I needed it. Charles hitched his boat and trailer to his pickup truck and backed it down a boat ramp. He released the winch and let his boat slide into the water. I took a line and pulled it to a slip and Dara secured it to the deck cleats. My boat was riding so low in the water that it took the combined effort of the three of us to pull it to Charles' trailer. Grenville watched us while we worked. Charles cranked the winch until Eagle Ray was nestled securely on the trailer and then he pulled her out of the water. Many gallons of seawater ran out of the hole in the hull as Charles pulled the sailboat to a vacant strip of concrete. With the water came small fish that had stowed away. Dara and I collected them and dropped them back into the Caribbean.

Charles was disconnecting the trailer when I asked, "How much do I owe you for the rental of your trailer?" Charles laughed, and said, "You don't owe nothing. You're a guest. Haven't you heard? We Bahamians are famous for our hospitality! In fact, why don't you two come to dinner at my house this evening?" I shook his hand and thanked him profusely. Dara said, "Yes, thank you, Charles!" Charles told us that we could find rooms at a place called the Morton Main House, and that he would pick us up there at seven, and then he returned to his office.

I'd been feeling dizzy ever since leaving the boat and it was getting worse. I sat down on the concrete and said, "I feel a little sick." If I'd had any food in my stomach, I'm sure that I would have thrown up. It had been five days since we'd departed Key West and I'd become accustomed to the constant motion. Now that I was back on land I was suffering a serious case of vertigo. I was breathing deeply in an effort to fight back the urge to dry-heave. I said, "This is embarrassing. I can't remember ever being seasick before." Dara said, "You're experiencing Mal de Debarquement Syndrome, and it's nothing to be embarrassed about. We'll find a store and get you a ginger ale. That'll help with the spins." I laid down on my back under the shade cast by my boat. From this vantage point, I could see the holes that I'd shot in the hull more clearly. They were surprisingly small and the damage looked like it would be fairly easy to repair. I'd assumed that I'd need a gallon of epoxy, a pint of hardener and several square feet of woven roving. But, from here, it looked like I could fix the hull with a simple repair kit. Luckily, the keel was undamaged.

The customs officer asked if I felt well enough to remove the salvage tube so that he could inspect my boat. I asked him to wait a few minutes so that my dizziness could pass. Dara said, "It's going to take longer than a few minutes for the spins to go away. I'll de-rig the salving gear." I explained how to deflate the tube without damaging it. Dara used the swim ladder to climb onboard. After she'd deflated the tube, she dragged it out of the boat and tossed it over the side. Grenville entered the cabin and conducted his inspection. Once he was satisfied that there was no contraband aboard, we filled out forms and he let us clear customs. I was thankful that he didn't make mention of my age in front of Dara. It cost $150 to enter the country by boat, but that included a cruising permit, a fishing permit, and the departure tax. I paid with three fifties that were still wet when I handed them to the customs officer. My working capital had dwindled to $1203 and whatever change might still be found in the boat.

Dara said that she was going to have a look around, and walked off toward Matthew Town. I was feeling a little better, so I went aboard my boat and climbed into the cabin so that I could check the damage. All of my books were soaked and unsalvageable. Saddest of all, my dictionary had melted into a reddish porridge. Everything was a mess, and there were dead fish everywhere. I hauled the cushions out of the V-berth and let them fall over the side of the boat. I hoped that they could be cleaned, but I wasn't sure. Without the cooling effect of the water around its hull, the boat's cabin had become extremely hot and that seemed to make the vertigo worse. I knew that I couldn't do much more cleaning without some supplies anyway, so I climbed out of the cabin and laid down in the cockpit under the Bimini and watched the world spin around me.

Half an hour later, Dara returned to the boat and called out, "Jamie, are you here?" I sat up and said, "Yeah. I'm up here." Dara climbed into the boat and handed me a can of something called Barritt's Ginger Beer. I cracked it open and took a sip. It was similar to ginger ale, but it tasted more strongly of ginger, and it had a subtle hint of honey. I didn't know if it would help with the vertigo, but it was cold and tasty. Dara said, "Jamie, I don't mean to be rude but for someone who loves the ocean as much as you clearly do, you don't seem to have much interest in the mechanics of sailing." I said, "I know that's a weakness of mine. It's just that I don't enjoy being on the water, as much as I enjoy being under it. The only place that feels like home is the world underwater. I don't feel completely like myself when I'm on the surface. Life underwater makes sense. Everything above it is just noisy, confusing and chaotic. Eagle Ray means the world to me, but if I could sleep underwater without drowning, I wouldn't need a boat." Dara said, "Well, your strength is freediving, and in my opinion that's causing you to neglect your sailing skills." I said, "You're right, and I will make that a priority. Either that, or get a powerboat."

Dara accepted that she'd made her point and so she changed the topic, "I reserved us rooms at the hotel." I asked,

"How much?" She said, "Not much. They only charge $108 a night." I asked, "For each room?" She said, "Of course. That's super cheap." For a moment I considered sleeping on the boat. Then I would only be out the money for Dara's room. But, I had been bitten by mosquitoes several times already, so I opted for the hotel. It was going to take two days for the epoxy to cure, and maybe three just to be safe. I was going to be out either $432 or $648 depending on how many days we stayed. Dara seemed to read my mind. She said, "It's likely that the directions will tell you to let it cure longer than you really need to, just for legal reasons. It would probably be safe to sail tomorrow." Dara was probably right. I'd learned enough about her to know that she wouldn't propose something like that if she didn't think it was safe. If I were alone, I might risk it. But, I wasn't alone. I was responsible for Dara's safety. I said, "Let's err on the side of caution and stay at least two days. I don't want to sink my boat twice in one week."

After an hour, the vertigo had more or less passed and so Dara and I walked to the Inagua General Store and bought trash bags, bleach, paper towels and a fiberglass repair kit. The cost of the supplies was under $50. I was eager to get started on the

174

repairs, so we headed straight back to the boat. We bagged up everything that had been destroyed by the water; my books, the old paper charts, the crushed water jugs and the dozen other things that couldn't stand up to the two atmospheres of seawater. I was happy to find that my Waterproof Chart #16 was in pristine condition. We threw the trash bags into a dumpster and then moved everything that might be saved off of the boat and onto the concrete pad. We found a water faucet and a hose and filled a 50 gallon drum with water. I dismounted my outboard and attached it to the inside of the drum so that I could run the motor a few times a day so that it wouldn't seize up due to the soaking it had taken. I knew that the service life of my outboard had been greatly reduced, but I was hoping that it would get me to PR. I would need to replace the electronic components before getting underway again.

My tools had already started to rust, so I submerged them in a bucket of freshwater to slow the oxidation process. I rinsed everything on the concrete pad with freshwater. I sprayed the cushions until they were water logged and then wrung them out and repeated the procedure several times. We hauled the hose onboard and washed down the interior of the cabin. I stuck the nozzle between the cabin sole and the hull and washed down the bilge. Dara found a bucket and mixed up some bleach water. We used that to wash down the interior again. Hopefully, that would prevent the growth of mold and neutralize the odor of any dead sea creatures that we might have missed. We turned our attention to the exterior of the boat. We raised the mainsail and unfurled the jib and washed them down with freshwater. We disconnected the mainsail from the boom and let the jib sheets dangle freely over the side of the boat so that the sails wouldn't catch the wind while they were drying. Next, we washed down the hull with freshwater and left her to dry.

At noon we walked to the hotel and had lunch. The hotel was painted white with green accents. The hotel room reminded me of an Old Florida motel near Crystal River where we'd stayed when Dad was still alive. The only item on the menu was fried chicken and fried potatoes. It was good, but it seemed great after eating canned tuna and soup for the better part of a week. I said to Dara, "I would really like to try some authentic Bahamian food." Dara said, "Oh, you're in for a treat. It's great! Don't worry. I'm sure that you can try some Bahamian cooking tonight when we go to Charles' house for dinner." I said, "Oh, yeah. That's right. I'd forgotten."

After lunch, we prepped the damaged hull and opened the repair kit and began applying the fiberglass and epoxy resin. The work went much more smoothly with two people. We took our time with the task. On the sea, Dara was all business, but now that we were back on land, her demeanor had changed. She seemed happier. She laughed and told jokes and was just fun to be around. Dara worked inside the cabin, while I worked on the outer hull. I heard her call from inside the boat, "Good news! I found one of your pickles floating in the bilge. You want to split it?" I said, "Heck, yeah! Bilge water pickles are the best!" She grabbed a lifeline and swung her body over the gunwale and did a twist in the air before landing on the concrete. She held her arms above her head and yelled, "Ten!" Then, she removed a pickle from the pocket of her sailing pants and shoved it in my face and said, "Here! Eat it!" I said, "You eat it. I dare you." Dara said, "Well, if it's a dare, I don't have much choice." She made a show of taking a tiny nibble from the pickle. She immediately spat it out and tossed the rest into the grass. She said, "Yuck! I think that we've both just learned something very important." I said, "What's that?" She said, "Don't eat food that you find in the bilge." I said, "I learn something new from you, every single day."

After a couple hours of curing, I sanded the fiberglass and applied more resin. Once we were satisfied that we'd done a decent job with the fiberglass, we turned our attention to the steering problem. We cleaned out the pieces of broken rudder that were still attached to the tiller. A rudder for my boat is a four hundred dollar part back home. Due to the law of supply and demand, I was sure that it would cost more here. We walked to the harbor master's office and found Charles speaking with some Jamaican men from a supply boat. We sat quietly on a bench and enjoyed the lyrical sounds of the Jamaican Patois. I couldn't tell you what they were talking about, but it was pleasant to listen to them, all the same.

After the men had gone, I approached Charles and asked him if he knew where I could buy a rudder for Eagle Ray. Charles frowned, but he also had a twinkle in his eye. He said, "We could call around the marine stores on New Providence and have one sent here on the mail boat." I said, "Whatever it takes." He smiled broadly and said, "But I got me a better idea." He led us outside to the slip where his Catalina was berthed. He said, "Why don't you just measure the rudder on my boat? I got some marine plywood I'm not using. You can use my tools to cut out a rudder, and then cover it with fiberglass." I said, "That would be amazing! Thank you again!" He showed me the plywood and loaned me a circular saw, a jig saw, and a coping saw. It only took an hour to get the wood worked into the shape that I wanted. I had to return to the store to get fiberglass roving, which set me back almost $50. But, that was a bargain compared to buying a new rudder. I took another hour to apply the fiberglass and I left it hanging from a rafter in Charles' workshop to cure.

It was getting late in the day, so Dara and I walked back toward town. All of our clothes were either soaked or filthy, so we stopped at a store along the way and bought some things to wear. I bought a couple of t-shirts and a pair of cargo shorts. Dara bought a long blue dress, and some sandals. After we got to the hotel, I went to my room and showered and changed. The power on the island was supplied by a diesel generator, and you could hear the sound of its engine in most parts of Matthew Town. The droning of the generator made me drowsy, so I set my alarm for 6:45 and laid down for a nap. When the alarm chimed, I had to struggle to wake up. I rolled over onto my stomach, pushed myself up and took long, deep breaths. The increased oxygen intake helped me come awake. I went to the bathroom and splashed my face with water and brushed my teeth. When I looked into the bathroom mirror, my facial hair looked as though it had grown an inch since I'd left Key West. Frankly, I was beginning to look a little like the pirate known as Blackbeard.

There was a knock on the door and I heard Dara say, "Hey, get a move on! I don't want to be late for dinner." I opened the door and the sight of her made my heart skip a beat. She was wearing a strapless, ankle-length cotton dress. It was tie-dyed with horizontal lines of blue and white. The blue accentuated her eyes. She had done something to her hair. It wasn't messy anymore. It was fancy now, like a style a fashion model would wear. She wasn't wearing make-up. She didn't need it, and it could only serve to mask her naturally pretty features. I was about to tell her that she was the most beautiful woman that I'd ever seen, but she spoke first, "What are you gawking at? Come on! Shake a leg!" Then, she turned and walked away. I locked the door and caught up to her in the parking lot. I wanted to say something nice. All that I could come up with was, "I like your perfume." She said, "Thanks! It's called soap. I'll buy you some if you promise to try it."

Charles picked us up around seven, give or take. Island time is flexible. He drove us to the south side of the island, just outside of Matthew Town and stopped at a two-story house that had to have been at least a hundred years old. It was painted white and aquamarine, with large open windows and verandas on all sides. We got out of the truck and Dara said, "You have a beautiful home." Charles said, "Thank you, Miss. I take great pride in keeping it maintained." It seemed as though the whole population of the island was present. I asked, "Is this a holiday?" Charles said, "Nah. We're a little out of the way, so we don't get to meet a lot of new people. Any time nice people come here, it's an excuse to throw a party."

The music was provided by a man and two ladies. The man was playing an accordion. One of the ladies was playing a handsaw, with a knife blade. The other lady was playing some kind of African-looking drum. She held it between her legs and beat it with her palms and fingers. The music was jaunty and upbeat, and many of the party goers were dancing to it. I said to Charles, "I like that music. What's it called?" Charles said, "We call it rake and scrape. The star of the show is the handsaw, and the beat comes from the goombay drum." I said, "I've never heard of Goom Bay. Is that in the Bahamas?" Charles laughed and said, "No, Brother. Goombay is a derivation of the Bantu word for a special kind of ceremonial drum. This music here speaks to our souls. And, you're fortunate, because tonight Nelson and his sisters are playing as a gift to their friends, for our enjoyment. When they play for tourists, it just ain't half as good. This music makes us feel a sense of community and togetherness. Can you feel it, Brother?" I said, "Yeah. I think I can feel it." But, I didn't really feel what he had described. I liked the music, but it didn't evoke any particular emotion, other than a vague sense of loneliness. I briefly wondered if there might be something wrong with me, but then decided to chalk it up to having lived in the U.S. for too long.

After an hour of energetic playing, Nelson and his sisters knocked off for the evening. Someone put on some Soca music, and people started moving toward the buffet tables. My mouth watered at the aromas that were wafting through the air. Charles directed us toward a line of folding tables that had been set up near a gumbo-limbo tree. The table held more conch than I'd ever seen in my life. There was raw conch, conch salad, conch fritters, cracked conch, and of course, conch chowder. Charles handed us plates and I tried a little of everything. Conch wasn't the only thing on the evening's menu. We had grouper, crawfish, and green turtle soup. The green turtle soup was a tasty stew with potatoes, carrots, okra, green pepper, celery, and tomatoes. There were plantains which were salty and excellent. I discovered my new favorite side dish that evening, peas and rice. The peas and rice had salt pork, tomato and hot peppers. So far, that has been the best meal that I've ever had.

Dara and I must have shook hands and chatted with at least a hundred people. I wasn't used to big parties like this, so I spent most of the evening hanging out on the periphery of the party and talking to Charles during the brief moments when he wasn't attending to his guests. Dara, on the other hand seemed to experience great pleasure each time that she met a new person. If I hadn't spent the past five, almost six days with her, and learned what a genuinely caring person she was, I would have sworn that she was working the room. Watching her, it was as though she had known the people at the party her whole life. Dara was laughing at other people's stories and telling stories of her own. She was like a lighthouse that people were attracted to, and it wasn't just because she was pretty. She just seemed to connect with people, and I think that was because she was genuinely interested in getting to know them. A little girl walked up to her and hugged her leg. Dara picked her up, said something to her that I couldn't make out, hugged her and then held the girl on her left hip while she continued her story. A stranger could easily have assumed, based on her body language, that she was the child's mother.

Charles tapped me on the shoulder and said, "Hey, boy. You look like you're thinking some deep thoughts." I pointed at the big shaggy red tree that was presiding over the festivities and said, "I was just wondering how old that gumbo-limbo tree is."

Charles laughed and said, "Sure, you was. You was staring right past that pretty girl and thinking about that tree." He laughed again and said, "Down here we call that the gamalamee tree. It's a blessing, that tree. You just boil the bark and you get medicine for nearly anything that ails you. It takes care of poisonwood, bites, cold, fever, and any number of problems that ain't been discovered yet. Besides that, this here's a holy tree. It's related to the same trees that give up the resins we call frankincense and myrrh." I said, "No kidding? I always wondered what frankincense and myrrh were." He said, "It's also related to balsa wood." I thought about that for a minute and then said, "So, the same type of medicinal tree is found in the middle east, the Bahamas, and in Peru. That's mind boggling." Charles said, "The world is full of mysteries. Indeed, it is."

Dara seemed to be telling an interesting story, because her new friends were laughing hysterically. I moved closer so that I could hear what she was saying. Balancing the little girl between the hollow of her left arm, and her hip, she spread her hands apart and said, "So, then he was standing there, just staring these thugs down, right? He had his arms open like he wanted to give them

185

all a big hug! And then, he's all like; Hey buddies, don't shoot me! I like drug dealers!" Laughter erupted from all around. Dara continued, "And these guys... These armed goons...They don't know what to make of this guy. They just scratch their heads and look at each other with these dumb expressions." I hoped that I was the hero in Dara's story, but I was afraid that I was going to be the butt of a joke, so I walked toward the sea and focused on the sound of the waves crashing until I was out of earshot of Dara's story.

The sun was going down, so I turned to the west to watch its progress across the horizon. Charles approached me and said, "How's it going, Brother?" I said, "It's great. I can't thank you enough for having us. You're a very generous man." He ignored the compliment and said, "That girl there, she thinks a lot of you. I know a thing or two about women. The time is going to come when you're gonna need to be bold. That girl there needs a bold fella. You just remember that."

I wasn't comfortable talking about Dara, so I changed the subject, "Your island is amazing. It's so unspoiled." Charles said, "We owe that to the Morton Salt Company." That explained the name of the hotel, Morton Main House. Charles said, "Most of Great Inagua is owned by Morton. They've been extracting salt from seawater there for more than sixty years. It's fair to say that Great Inagua is worth its weight in gold. If you ever find a high-rise resort here, you'll know it's a sign that the apocalypse is close at hand." I asked, "How many people live here?" Charles said, "I'm not sure. Man, woman and baby, I think it's between eight hundred and a thousand. You've met most of the people this night." I said, "I envy you. This is an amazing place to live." Charles said, "I envy you. You've got your whole life ahead of you, and I can see that you're a traveler. Me, myself, I've never left the Bahamas. I yearn to see something new, but I probably never will." Around midnight, Charles drove us back to the hotel. My exhaustion, combined with the droning of the generator made me sleep like a rock.

The next morning, Dara and I walked to Government Dock to check on my boat. Inagua possessed two characteristics that distinguished it from any other place that I'd been. The first was the mountainous piles of salt that had been extracted from the sea. The second was the more than 80,000 flamingoes that populated the island. A flock of at least a thousand flamingoes flew over our heads and, in my worst Cuban accent, I said, "Dara, look at the pelican fly! Come on, pelican!" Dara said, "Those are flamingoes, not pelicans." I said, "I know. I was doing Tony Montana." She said, "What?" I said, "I was doing a line from that old movie, *Scarface*." Dara said, "Never heard of it." I gasped, "Are you kidding me? It's a classic! Al Pacino plays a cocaine trafficker from Havana." Dara said, "Sorry, still never heard of it." I said, "Have you ever heard anyone use the phrase; Say hello to my little friend?" She said, " Yeah, brain-damaged frat boys say that when they're drunk." I felt embarrassed, so I just said, "Well, it was still a good movie." Dara said, "Ugh. I will never understand why guys find that kind of stuff entertaining."

When we reached Government Dock, we looked the boat over and found that the fiberglass had cured. I said, "So, what do you think?" Dara said, "It looks good to me. We could shove off tomorrow morning, if you want." I said, "It would be nice to stay another day, but my funds are pretty tight." She said, "You're paying for the rooms, so it's up to you." I said, "Alright, it's agreed. We'll leave tomorrow." We climbed aboard and found that everything that we'd left on the boat was still there. My sea anchor had dried, so we folded it and stowed it in a cockpit locker. My salvage tubes were draped across the boat. I licked the salvage tubes and they tasted salty, so I washed them down with freshwater again. Dara laughed and said, "I thought that I was the only one who tasted her gear." I said, "How else will you know if you've got all of the salt off?" She said, "I know, right? But, people still think that I'm weird when they see me doing it." I said, "I don't think that you're weird." Dara said, "Oh, Thank you! That's the nicest thing that anyone has ever said to me."

I asked, "What day is this?" Dara looked at her phone and said, "Today is Wednesday, the 27th." I realized that I hadn't contacted my mom for more than a week. My phone was charging in my room, so I asked Dara if I could use her phone to send an email. She handed me the phone and said, "Swipe the screen in an L shape to unlock it." When I opened my email account, there were at least thirty messages from Mom. I was feeling guilty, so I didn't read them. I just composed a new message. I thought that it would be reassuring if I kept it breezy and casual, "Dear Mom, I hope that everything is going well. I'm in the Bahamas right now, but I'll be in Culebra within two weeks. Please contact the family and let them know that I'm on my way. Also, do you know where the key for the house is now? I know that it used to be in that one place in the shed. Anyway, write soon. Love ya!"

I handed the phone back to Dara and said, "Thank you." She said, "No problem. Let's go diving." I said, "That sounds great. What do you have in mind?" She said, "Last night at the party, Charles said that we could borrow that dinghy in his workshop." I said, "I saw it, too. It doesn't have a motor." She said, "I know, but you do." I said, "Good thinking! Let's hook it up." The dinghy was an RIB, which stands for Rigid Inflatable Boat. They're very light and a lot of fun to drive. We carried the boat to the water and then mounted my outboard. Dara grabbed our gear and put it into the small boat. I carried my air cylinders to the shop and filled them with Charles' compressor. It was a small compressor that only filled at a rate of 3 cubic feet per minute, so it took nearly an hour to fill both cylinders.

While we waited, we picked Charles' brain for dive locations and things to do. He told us that if we brought back some conch, he would make conch chowder for lunch. But, he told us that it was illegal to use scuba gear to harvest either fish or shellfish. He showed us a map of the island and pointed to a spot a few hundred yards from shore. He said, "This is the area that we're harvesting from now. The bottom is about six feet. Conchs don't live deeper than forty feet, and we're on a ledge that drops off to nine-hundred feet pretty quickly. Look for the red algae that grow on turtle grass and soft coral. That's what Mr. Conch likes to eat. Don't take more than ten conchs each." Charles showed us a mature conch shell, so that we would not take a juvenile by mistake. He said, "It takes five years for a conch to get old enough to make baby conch, so only take the biggest ones." Dara looked at me and said, "I guess we should unload the scuba gear." I asked Charles, "Can I leave my air cylinders in your workshop for now?" He said, "That's no problem. Just don't forget them when you leave." We stowed the scuba gear on Eagle Ray and then headed out with our snorkeling gear and a wet gunny sack to keep the conch in. As we were casting off, Charles said, "Don't throw any empty conch shells into the water. Empty shells make the harvest a pain in the backside." That explained why there were so many empty conch shells lying around the island.

We spent the morning snorkeling. The marine life wasn't spectacular compared to the dive off of Anguilla Cays, but the conchs were plentiful. We didn't want to be greedy, so we only took three each. We brought the dinghy back to the marina at noon and Charles made us all chowder for lunch. We spent the afternoon provisioning Eagle Ray. This time, I bought a radio. It was second hand, so it only set me back $90. I bought a small can of marine paint and repainted the hull where we'd made the repair. The off-white color didn't exactly match the rest of the hull, but it was below the waterline, so I didn't spend much time trying to make it pretty. I serviced my outboard and replaced its electronic components. My tools were in bad shape, so I replaced the ones I could and covered the rest with a coat of motor oil. I lost the receipt, so I'm not sure how much I spent on the parts and tools. It was more than $80, because when I counted my money, I only had $500 left. But, that didn't matter because Eagle Ray was seaworthy again.

Early the next morning, Charles launched Eagle Ray and then we helped him load his Catalina back onto its trailer. I retrieved my air cylinders and stowed them on my boat. Charles shook my hand and gave Dara a hug and said, "You come back soon, okay?" We said that we definitely would try, and we thanked him again for his hospitality. Then, we conducted one last inventory of the boat, and got underway. Dara manned the tiller until we were clear of shallow water and boat traffic. I found my log and made an entry, "Day 13: May 28th. We departed Great Inagua. We're heading southeast toward San Juan. We are approximately 300 miles from Puerto Rican waters. Our ETA to landfall on Culebra is 3 to 4 days."

After two hours of sailing, we encountered an armada of poachers heading north from Haiti and the Dominican Republic toward the Great Bahama Bank. Neither I nor Dara felt comfortable with the boat traffic, so we bore off a little to the east, on a heading that would eventually take us across Silver Bank and to the north of Navidad Bank. The boat traffic eased up, and we only occasionally crossed paths with other cruisers. Several of them heaved-to, I assume so that we could chat and compare notes. But, we were on the last leg of our journey and we both had "barn fever," so we just waved and slipped on by without stopping.

Dara had taken the six-to-ten watch, and I'd taken the ten to two. At the end of her second watch at six in the evening, Dara heaved-to and dropped sails. We had made nearly sixty miles so far, and we were lying about halfway between Grand Caicos to the north, and Ile de la Tortue, Haiti to the south. At our current location, the sea bottom lay 12,000 feet below us, so anchoring was impossible. Instead, we just drifted for a little while. Dara said, "Let's take a break and have a civilized supper." She disappeared into the cabin for a moment and then returned with a plastic container full of peas and rice, and plantains. Dara said, "A gift from Charles! He said that you owe him a debt, and that is to always remember the hospitality of the people of Inagua." Dara and I didn't bother splitting up the food into separate plates. We each just took a fork and dug in. After we'd finished our meal, I went into the cabin to get us some water. Standing in the cabin, I suddenly became aware of a deep throbbing vibration and the sound of a high pitched whine. An exceptionally powerful boat was closing with us.

I climbed into the cockpit and said, "Another boat's coming up on us fast." Dara reached into the cabin, pulled out my binos and scanned the horizon until she fixed on something off of the starboard beam. She handed me the binos and sat down without a word. I looked through the binoculars, and even though they were at least half a mile away, I could tell that it was Simpatico. Dara said, "Maldonado is going to want revenge for what you did to his man." I was terrified. Not for myself, but for her. I said, "Dara, I'm so sorry that I got you into this." She said, "What are you talking about? I chose your boat, remember?" That was true, but it didn't make me feel any better.

Dara disappeared into the cabin for a moment and retrieved her sun hat, a tube of sunscreen, and a few important documents that she placed into plastic bags and then shoved into the bikini top underneath her shirt. She looked at me and said, "You should probably stow your ID cards in your underwear. If they don't kill us, you might need them. Also, you're going to want a hat." I felt rage toward Maldonado at that moment. The bravest woman I'd ever met in my life was just accepting as a given fact that she would once again be set adrift by the man. I followed Dara's suggestion regarding my driver's license and passport card.

The Donzi was moving at incredible speed, at least a hundred miles an hour. When they backed off the throttle, the boat came off plane and created massive waves that stopped all of Eagle Ray's forward momentum. Seawater washed over the gunwales. The weight of the water forced Eagle Ray's cockpit down toward the surface of the sea, and I feared that she'd be swamped and sink. I began to appreciate how much thought had gone into my boat's design when I saw the mass of seawater drain out through the transom, instead of into the cabin. The wind was gone, so Dara lowered the mainsail and furled the jib.

Simpatico orbited Eagle Ray, in ever smaller concentric circles. This time, there were only three men. It was just Maldonado and two others from the previous encounter. Jaime was absent. When they got close enough that I could see their faces, I recognized astonishment. That may have been why they didn't fire their guns in the air this time. Simpatico pulled alongside and the men lashed their boat to Eagle Ray. Maldonado said, "Dara! It gives me great pleasure to see that you are alive and well!" Dara said, "Thank you, sir. I would like to stay that way." Maldonado said, "Dara, you wound me. You and I are old acquaintances. You must surely know that I would never harm you." He was clearly trying to play the part of the kindly uncle, but he didn't quite pull it off.

Maldonado turned his attention to me. From his sneer, I could tell that it did not give him pleasure to see that I was alive and well. He said, "Ah! It's my amigo! It's the one who likes comunistas y narcotraficantes! Do you have something clever to say now?" Dara was pleading with her eyes. They said, "Jamie, please stop being you." She was right, and her safety was my first concern. I shook my head and said, "No. I don't have anything to say." Maldonado said, "Good! You've learned humility. If you continue to behave like a gentleman, then I might put you on the balsa with Dara." From the look in his eyes, and the evil grins that his men were exchanging, I was sure that he was lying, probably to put us off guard.

I decided to play along and said, "Mr. Maldonado, I apologize for my rudeness." Maldonado said, "First, you may address me as Captain. Second, tell me what you intend to do about the injuries you um...did to my associate, Jaime?" I said, "Captain, I deeply regret harming your friend and I hope that you will extend him my apologies." I was trying to think of something to say that would mollify the man so that he might spare Dara's life. It was weak tea, but I said, "I would like to pay for his medical bills." Maldonado said, "Oh, you will."

He gestured to his men and they leapt onboard Eagle Ray. The two men shoved me onto the deck and lashed my hands together with plastic cable ties. They stood me upright and then one of the men backhanded me across my right cheek. The blow stung my face, but not nearly as much as it stung my pride, and I was angrier than I'd ever been before. I remembered the words of Jesus, "Whosoever shall smite thee on thy right cheek, turn to him the other." I turned my left cheek to the man and said, "Hey! Cabrón! I'm a man! You want to hit me? You better hit me like a man!" I expected him to punch me with his right fist, but instead he backhanded me again with his left. The two men laughed as they jostled me over the gunwales and onto Simpatico and shoved me into a smallish space between the pilots' chairs and the line of seats that abutted the engine compartment. I sat up so that I could see what would become of Dara. I expected them to shove me back down, but they were busy now and ignoring me for the moment. I climbed up onto the rear seats, and they either didn't notice or didn't care.

Maldonado was true to his word in regard to Dara. The pirates put a life raft into the water and loaded it with an EPIRB unit, a five gallon can of water and what looked like military rations. Maldonado was standing on Eagle Ray, speaking to Dara in a greasy tone, "Don't worry about your friend. We won't hurt him. We just want to explain things to him so that he doesn't make the same mistake again." Dara remained silent, so Maldonado simply gestured Dara toward the life raft. Without a word, she hopped off of Eagle Ray and into the raft. The man had broken Dara's spirit, if only temporarily, and for the first time in my life, I felt hatred for another human being. Maldonado untied the line securing the raft, tossed it into the water and said, "Vaya con Dios!" He didn't look at Dara again. It was as though she had ceased to exist. I locked eyes with Dara as the raft floated away. I was terrified for her. I could tell that she was terrified also, and I hoped that it wasn't for me. She needed to focus on her own survival. She was floating away in a tiny boat on a great big ocean. I prayed that someone would find her soon.

The men chatted while they searched my boat. One of the men found our phones and pocketed them. After the previous sinking, I'd squirreled my money away in that pickle jar, and wedged it into a small space between the starboard cockpit locker and the hull. I doubted that it would make a difference to me, but I felt a little satisfaction that they hadn't found my cash. From listening to the conversation, I learned that the man who had backhanded me was named Martin and the other went by his surname Cami. Cami, the man who had taken the phones, gestured to Maldonado with my binoculars and said in Spanish, "Malo! May I keep this for my kid?" Maldonado nodded. I said, in broken Spanish, "Filtrar Especial! Mirar al Sol!" He tried it, and then cried out as the sun's rays burned his eyes. Martin jumped from Eagle Ray to Simpatico and backhanded me a couple of times, but it was worth it. Dara was not in immediate danger, so I didn't have to be nice to these animals anymore. Cami recovered quickly enough and I expected him to punch me or something, but he just ignored me and went on with his job. Something about his cold detachment made me think that he was much more dangerous than Martin. I guessed that if they decided to kill me, Cami would be the one to do it. Once they were satisfied that there was nothing of real value onboard, the men set to work rigging a towing bridle.

A towing bridle is shaped like two letter Ys, joined at the base. The bridle keeps the bow of the boat being towed from turning away to the port or starboard. They attached one end of the bridle to the primary winches of my sailboat and the other end to cleats on Simpatico. Then they raised the rudder and cast off the lines that had secured the two boats. Maldonado took the helm and engaged the transmission. We started moving forward slowly and he kept an eye on Eagle Ray. It was clear that Maldonado didn't trust that his men possessed the finesse required for the job. We motored east at ten knots. That must have seemed maddeningly slow to the men who were accustomed to the power of the Donzi, but it was the fastest speed that my own boat had ever reached. Maldonado must have become satisfied that everything was rigged properly, because he had stopped looking aft to check on Eagle Ray.

The pirates continued to ignore me, and I wondered when the beatings would begin. I thought that, if I was lucky, they might just shoot me in the head and toss me overboard. An hour later, at dusk, Maldonado must have become bored with his mundane task, because he muttered something to Martin who dragged me forward and dropped me into the seat next to Maldonado. He said, "Mijo, I assume that you survived last time because you had the...um what do you call the thing for the pesca submarina?" I said, "Scuba gear." He said, "Ah! That's right! I remember the word from the *Sea Hunt*." I had a hard time believing that a professional smuggler didn't know the English name for scuba gear.

The man was clumsily trying to build a rapport, and I knew that he was fishing for information. He said, "What I would like to know is how you got your boat off of the bottom of the sea." I said, "I sometimes do salvage work. I had a couple of sea salvage tubes on board." The light reflecting off of the instrument panel revealed a sly gleam in Maldonado's eyes. He said, "That was very resourceful of you. From now on, I'm going to have my transports carry this type of equipment. Mijo, you may have just saved me a great deal of money." I decided to stall for time. I said, "I have a lot of great ideas. Maybe I could do some consulting for you. My rates are reasonable." Maldonado clipped and lit a cigar and simply said, "No. While, I appreciate your youthful enthusiasm, I'm sure that you do not have the...um...aptitude for the profession." He pulled a package of chewing gum from his left breast pocket and asked, "Chicle?" I said, "No thank you. My dentist recommends against it." He chuckled and said, "You're good company. You know that? Say something else that's funny." I didn't really want to entertain the man who was going to kill me, but I was desperate to buy some time. I said, "I don't know if this is funny or not, but my name is Jaime." Maldonado laughed uproariously, slapped his knee and said, "That explains the stupid look on your face when I ordered Jaime to board your balsa!" I didn't care for the fact that Maldonado referred to my sailboat as a raft.

I said, "We seem to be hitting if off, so I hate to ruin the mood, but what's it going to be? A bullet?" Maldonado was silent for moment and then said, "I think that I will let Jaime decide." Martin and Cami were playing dominoes in the cabin. Maldonado called to them in Spanish, "One of you men, bring me the telephone, please." Cami came on deck and handed Maldonado an Iridium satellite phone and a small black address book. It was smart of them not to save numbers in the phone. If they were boarded, the address book would be easier to destroy or hide than a sat-phone.

Maldonado punched in the other Jaime's phone number and held the phone against his right ear. A few moments passed and then Maldonado dialed a second time. He said apologetically, "He is slow to answer." Finally, someone picked up and Maldonado began a conversation in Spanish, "How are you Marisol? Yes, I would be happy to come to dinner, but not this weekend. I have work. I am disappointed, too. I was calling to check on Jaime. Can he talk?" He pressed the phone against his chest and said, "I'm sorry, but it will just be a moment. Jaime is making his toilet. His wife is taking him the phone." Maldonado raised the phone to his ear and, after a brief silence said, "Jaime! I have some good news for you. We have found the young caballero who injured you." I could hear an excited whoop through the phone's speaker. Maldonado pulled it away from his ear and spoke into the microphone, "Jaime, calm down. I just called to ask you what you would like us to do with him." I heard a flurry of excited Spanish that I couldn't quite make out. Maldonado said, "Jaime, calm down. I would like to bring him to you but that is not practical. Just tell me what you would like to happen, and I will make it happen."

Maldonado listened briefly and then said, "Thank you, Jaime. I have to go now. Yes, I will take photos. Yes, and video, too. Goodbye." Maldonado ended the call and then said, "Jaime requests that we break your knees, cover your body with the juice of the poisonwood tree, and then leave you to bake in the sun for a few hours. After that, he would like us to shoot you in the face." Aside from my fear for Dara's safety; I was more deeply frightened than I could remember ever having been. I'd screwed up and I wanted to get out of this situation in the least painful way that I could manage. I said, "Why not just shoot me in the face now and

205

just tell Jaime that you did all of the other stuff?" Maldonado said, "Madre de Dios! That would be lying! I had assumed that you were an honorable man. I am shocked that you would even suggest such a thing!"

Maldonado had a changeable mood and within an instant he seemed to have become bored with our conversation. He ordered me tossed back on the deck just aft of the pilot's seat. It was as though he had determined that my fate was sealed and that my presence was no longer important enough to acknowledge. I wasn't sure why they hadn't broken my knees yet. Maybe they still needed me to be able to walk somewhere. If so, they were planning to take care of me on land. I had as much time as it would take them to reach their destination. I considered jumping overboard, but if they saw me or noticed that I was gone soon enough, they would just turn around and pick me up. I could stay underwater until they gave up and left, but then I would be adrift with little more than luck to impel me toward land.

Martin had tossed me down next to the starboard cleat that held one of the bridle lines. The pirates were not careful with their garbage. There were beer cans, cigar butts, and many other types of litter strewn across the deck. Nothing looked useful, except for a plastic first-aid kit that was lying behind the passenger pilot's seat. I scooted close to it and pulled it behind my back. With my arms bound, it wasn't easy to open the kit. I felt for something sharp, hoping to find a razor blade. Instead, I struck gold. I felt the unmistakable shape of a pair of trauma shears. It took a few moments, but I was finally able to slide an edge of a shear under the plastic of the cuffs. I used the weight of my hips against the deck for leverage and the right side of the cuffs popped off. Maldonado must have heard the snap of the plastic being cut, because he began turning in his seat. Thanks to his girth, he turned slowly enough that I was able to lie down on the deck and pretend to be asleep. He only watched me for a moment before turning back to the wheel.

I didn't have much time to execute my plan, so I didn't bother with the left side of the cuff. I used the shears to cut the starboard, and then the port bridle lines and then slipped across the engine cover and jumped over the transom and swam as fast as I could for Eagle Ray. The power of the Donzi was so great that Maldonado had obviously not even felt my boat come free, because he kept motoring along at ten knots. I reached the bow of my boat and slid along the hull until I caught the swim ladder. Once onboard, I gathered up the towing bridle and tossed it overboard. I started the outboard and then followed the back azimuth of the one we'd been following. If I were left alone, I guessed that I might be able to find Dara in two to three hours. If the EPIRB that Maldonado had given her functioned, the Coast Guard would be broadcasting a request for assistance with her GPS coordinates on Channel 16.

Before I had time to retrieve my radio, I heard Simpatico's engines throttle up and then I heard the whoosh of water as she made a quick turn. Two spotlights shone on my boat as the Donzi pulled alongside Eagle Ray for the third time. Maldonado was holding an old fashioned revolver. It was the kind that you've seen in westerns. He said, "I've changed my mind, I'm going to honor your request and just tell Jaime that we did as he asked. It's only a little white lie and it will save me so much trouble. Besides, I owe this kindness to you for telling me about how to raise the sunken boats." He aimed the gun at me, but before he could cock it, I went over the side. I swam under Eagle Ray and grabbed onto her keel. I saw spotlights cutting through the water on both sides of my boat, but I didn't think that the beams could reach me where I was. I heard feet stomping along the deck and companionway, and muffled yells. They were waiting for me to surface, and I could see that they were shining their lights farther from the boat with each passing minute. I hoped that they didn't have another bridle and that they would just leave Eagle Ray to drift.

After fifteen minutes they stopped searching with their lights and started moving around the deck. I swam to the far side of Simpatico and surfaced so that I could hear better. Maldonado was showing the two men how to jury-rig a towing bridle. I swam to the Donzi's transom and peeked around just long enough to see that all three men were onboard Eagle Ray. The Donzi's engine was still running and I knew that I had one shot at escape. I hauled myself aboard, ran to the wheel, put the transmission in forward and pushed the throttle to full. The Donzi's bow leapt out of the water, breaking all but one of the lines holding her to the smaller boat. My eyes were focused forward as I tried to gain control of the dragon on whose back I'd just leapt. I heard, but didn't see my boat capsize. It was a sickening, violent sound. The Donzi leapt forward after the last line broke. I slowed the engine and chanced a look back, but none of the men had made it onboard Simpatico. When I was sure that I was far enough away, I turned and made a circle. I turned on a spotlight and saw Eagle Ray righting herself. I thanked God that even though she was swamped, she was still afloat. I could see Maldonado in the water, but not the other men. They might have been floating on the other side of my boat, or they might have drowned.

I would have liked to have worked on taking my boat back, but I had a more important problem to deal with. I took up the heading where I hoped I would find Dara. I turned on the radio and an official-sounding female voice said, "Pan-Pan, Pan-Pan, Pan-Pan. All ships, all ships, all ships. This is United States Coast Guard Sector San Juan. All ships, be on the lookout for a vessel in distress." I was surprised to be picking up a signal from so far away, but whether it was an atmospheric anomaly or retransmission buoys, I felt fortunate. I thought that it was unlikely that the Coast Guard would venture this far from U.S. territorial waters for an EPIRB signal with no accompanying Mayday call. I guessed that they would rely on private vessels to render assistance instead. I wrote down the GPS coordinates for the BOLO and entered them into the GPS, and then followed the new, more accurate heading. Simpatico had covered ten miles over the past hour, but it would take a fraction of that time for her to get back to the spot where Dara had been set adrift.

A crescent moon reflected dimly off of a sea as smooth as glass, so I opened the throttle to half. The GPS indicated that I was doing 70 mph. I moved the throttle up another third and the speed increased to 105 mph. I said, "Oh! Ho! Ho!" as I opened the throttle two-thirds, and the speed increased to 140 mph! This was not a normal boat. It wasn't even a normal Donzi. This boat obviously had been modified beyond the manufacturer's specifications. This boat had super powers. After thirteen of the most exhilarating minutes of my life, I reached the vicinity of the GPS coordinates and throttled down and cut the engine. I didn't want Dara to think that Maldonado had returned to torment her again, so I walked to the bow and began calling, "Dara! Hey, Dara Kemm! Are you there?" From several yards away I heard Dara call out softly, "Yeah. It's me."

I shined the light to starboard and found her sitting in the raft. I fired up the Donzi and pulled it alongside her, put the transmission in neutral and tossed her a line. We pulled together until the raft was near enough to lash to the Donzi. She took both of my hands, and placed a steadying foot against the gunwale, and I pulled her onboard. I was about to ask if she was okay, but before I could, Dara grabbed the back of my head with her left hand, and pressed her lips against mine. Blood rushed to my head and my vision blurred. Heat radiated from my skin and I knew that I was turning bright red. I'm not exaggerating when I tell you that I literally, not figuratively, saw stars. I might have had a hallucination. Surely, the neurons in my brain were firing like machine guns. That may have interfered with my vision. Regardless, sharing that kiss was the warmest, most human feeling that I had ever experienced. She broke off the kiss and I sat down in the pilot's chair. I struggled to find words. I said, "That was... That was..." She said, "Don't read too much into it. I'd kiss anyone who'd get me off that raft."

Dara and I pulled the life raft onboard Simpatico and then I set my boat's last location as the destination in the GPS and got underway. This time, I kept the Donzi at the reasonable speed of 100 miles per hour. Dara said, "Where are we heading?" I explained how I'd escaped from Maldonado and his men and then I said, "I want to see if my boat's salvageable." Dara said, "I don't think that's a good idea. Those drug runners are going to want their cigarette boat back. They may still have their guns. Those things don't stop working just because they get wet." I said, "Let's just take a look. It's been in my mind to leave Maldonado in his life raft, and report his location to the authorities." Dara said, "That's awfully generous considering those guys were going to kill you a few minutes ago." I said, "It's not for them, it's for me. I know they're murderers, but I'm not." Dara said, "If you're set on doing this, then I'm going to go below and find a weapon." Dara rummaged around the cabin and checked all of the storage areas. She returned with a flare gun and a few vials of white powder. She said, "I guess that they were minimalists. I found cartridges, but no guns." I asked, "Is that cocaine?" She said, "I think so. Did you know that this stuff used to be legal? They used to sell it in drug stores and put it in soda-pop." I said, "Well, it's not legal anymore. We'd better get rid of it." Without a word, she tossed the vials into the ocean.

In fifteen minutes, we were back at the location where I'd swamped Eagle Ray. Dara stood on the bow and shined the spot light in every direction. There was no sign of my boat or Maldonado and his crew. Dara said, "What do you think? Do you think that they could have sailed your boat after it barrel-rolled?" I said, "I don't know. She was afloat, but just barely when I saw her last, and her rigging was a mess. It's been half an hour, so they may have floated away on the current. Most people can float in seawater. If they couldn't make it to my boat, they're probably bobbing around somewhere out there." Dara said, "They're not people. They're monsters. I hope they drown." I said, "I hope that no one finds them and picks them up. That would be really bad."

Dara said, "I'm sorry about your boat, Jamie." I said, "I'm sorry about your scuba gear." I did a quick tally in my head and I estimated that each of us was out about two grand. She moved into the co-pilot's chair and from there, the light from the cabin shone on my face. I wiped a drop of sweat away from my eye, and she asked, "Are you crying?" I said, "No." She said, "It's alright if you are. It's to be expected after a stressful situation. You were almost killed by pirates." I said, "I wasn't crying, Dara. But, if I had been, it wouldn't have been because of pirates. It would have been because Eagle Ray meant a lot to me and now she's gone." Dara said, "Oh! That actually makes sense." I said, "But, I wasn't crying. I don't cry." She said, "Fine, I believe you."

I widened the view on the GPS screen and tapped the location of Culebra, and set it as my destination. I said, "I know that you wanted to go to San Juan, but would you be willing to go to Culebra first?" Dara said, "I guess that's okay. I've never been there, and I've heard the diving isn't bad. But, don't you think it would be best to go to San Juan first and turn over this boat to the Coast Guard?" I said, "No. I'm keeping the boat." Dara said, "You can't keep the boat, Stupid. It's evidence." I said, "How is it evidence? Even if Maldonado is still alive and he somehow gets himself arrested, how is some lawyer showing a picture of this boat to the jury going to help anything? If we turn the boat in, they'll just auction it off and use the money for some wasteful government nonsense." Dara said, "Assuming he's still alive, turning this boat in could help bring Maldonado to justice." I said, "You want to talk about justice? This is justice; an eye for an eye, a tooth for a tooth, and a boat for a boat."

Dara said, "You know how I feel about Maldonado, but this boat is well known to law enforcement throughout the Caribbean, and we're not in Cuban waters anymore. If we get boarded, you must tell the truth about why we're aboard her, and if you won't, I will. You need to understand something, Jamie. I appreciate you saving my life, and I owe you." I said, "You don't owe me anything." She said, "Shut up and listen to me. I will never spend one minute of my life behind lock and key, not ever, not anywhere, and not for anyone. Not even for you." I'm embarrassed to admit this, but she was so vehement that she was scaring me a little bit. I simply said, "Understood." Dara said, "Good. We're in one accord." I said, "We're also in one really fast boat!"

The fuel tanks were nearly full, and we had a little more than 400 miles to traverse. It was a little after eight, and I hoped to make it to Culebra sometime the next morning. Neither of us had any experience with a speedboat of this caliber, but Dara said that if we wanted to make it without refueling in the Dominican

Republic or the north coast of Puerto Rico, we should keep the boat at around 50 MPH. For the first couple of hours, we jostled each other over control of the wheel. Piloting a Donzi at any speed is unspeakably fun and neither of us wanted to surrender a minute at the helm. By ten that night, fatigue had set in and we took turns driving the boat and sleeping in 30 minute shifts.

I hate to admit it, but the Donzi was much more comfortable than my Catalina. For one thing, the air-conditioner kept the cabin at a pleasant 85 degrees. Excitement impelled me to spend time rummaging around my new boat, when I should have been sleeping. I found a few items of contraband of the narcotic variety, and they went overboard.

On a hunch, I pulled up the carpet from the cabin sole and removed the hatches that access the bilge. I laid on my stomach and felt around until I found a dry-bag. The bag contained two hand grenades and two small blocks of what looked like modeling clay, and bore the marking, "C-4" on its cover. There was also a small box containing what looked like little metal firecrackers. The box was labeled, "Caps, Blasting." There was also some fuse cord and a box marked, "M-60 Fuse Igniters." I knew that having explosives onboard could turn out bad for me, in any number of ways, but for some reason that I'm not certain of, I returned the items to the dry-bag and stashed it back in the bilge.

I finished my survey and decided that besides smelling like cigar smoke, picadillo, and stale beer, the boat was in fairly pristine condition. I slept until six in the morning when Simpatico slowed and Dara called into the cabin, "Jamie! Wake up and pilot us in." I stepped on deck, took over the wheel, and set our speed at 20 miles per hour. We slid between Culebra and the island of Cayo Norte, and then later, past Culebrita. I stood off of the point called Cabeza de Perro and once clear of the shallows, covered the last two thousand feet of the two week journey.

Chapter Six

Most of the land that comprises the southeast corner of Culebra is a wildlife preserve. One of the few private residences on that peninsula is owned by a devastatingly handsome rogue named Jamie Bonifacio. At least, I would be the owner in twelve months. According to the terms of Dad's will, it wouldn't be mine, legally, until I turned eighteen. Until then, it was technically my mother's property.

I motored up to my private pier and idled alongside while Dara tied us off. I killed the engines and stepped onto the dock. I looked at Dara and said, "It's weird. I thought that I would feel different once I got here, but I feel the same as always." She said, "That's the thing about traveling. No matter where you go, there you are." I said, "Is that a quote from somebody?" She said, "It must have been." I said, "I think that you might be suffering from early morning silly talk." Dara said, "I do need some sleep." The sun hadn't risen, so I pointed up the dock and said, "My house is up there, about fifty yards. You should follow me." I shined a flashlight along the ground and Dara followed close behind. The house was really just a small bungalow constructed of cinder blocks. When we arrived, I shined my light across the front of the house and was happy to see that it was in superb condition. It had recently been painted a bright yellow, with pastel green accents. Dara said, "Nice place. Are you sure that this is your house?" I said, "Yes, ma'am."

I hadn't been back to the family house since Dad's funeral. It hadn't made sense for the entire family to fly to Sarasota, and even if they had, finding hotel rooms for them during tourist season would have been impossible. So, we'd flown Dad home and interred him in our little family cemetery. I'd kept in touch with my father's brother Felix through email and frequent phone calls. He'd retired from the Army about the same time that my dad passed away. He'd enlisted in the Army as a Private. He started out as a light-wheeled vehicle mechanic and ended up a Warrant Officer, running motor pools. After he retired, he moved home and bought a boat yard. The last time that we'd spoken, he told me that he was taking care of the house and that the family occasionally stayed there on the weekends.

I knocked on the door, and called out, "Hello! Felix! Is anybody home?" I waited for a response. Dara said, "I thought you said that this was your house." I said, "It is, but there might be relatives using it." No one answered me, and no lights came on, so I said, "Wait here, I'm going to the shed to try to find the key." Dara sat down in a wicker chair, and I walked around the corner of the house and into the shed. My dad's old 1967 International Scout was still parked in the shed. The last time that I'd seen it, it had been resting on concrete blocks. Uncle Felix had obviously been working on it, because now it had tires and rims. The hood was up and there was a charger attached to the battery, set to trickle. The body was rusty and needed some TLC and a paint job, but still it looked cool. I opened the door of the cab and found the house key in the ashtray. I also found an old packet of Juicy Fruit gum. My dad used to chew it to hide his cigar smoking from my mom. It never worked. There was one stick of gum left. I opened it and put it in my mouth, but it was so dry that it disintegrated almost instantaneously. The cab of the Scout still held the lingering scent of cigars that had been smoked long ago.

I walked back to the porch and unlocked the door. I shined the light around the living room, and found that everything seemed clean and orderly. So, I turned on the lights and checked out the rest of the rooms, just to make sure that no one was in the house. My little house had a living room, a kitchen, two bedrooms, and a bathroom. There was also a utility room that had been built on some time in the 1980s to accommodate a washer and dryer. I showed Dara to the larger bedroom and said, "You can take this room. There may be some clothes in the wardrobe, but I'm not sure. There's a washing machine out back." She collapsed on the bed and said, "I'm just going to rack out now and worry about that other stuff later. Can you turn off the light on your way out?" I said, "Sweet dreams." I don't think that she heard me, because she'd started snoring even before I'd flipped the light switch.

I'd been sleeping during Dara's watch, so I wasn't nearly as tired as she was. I wandered around the house for a while, looking at old family photos until I got sleepy. I took a shower and then put on a bathing suit and a t-shirt that I'd found in an old cedar chest. The clothes smelled of moth balls, which I found unpleasant. I dropped my dirty laundry into the washer but I decided to wait until Dara was up, and then do one load. I was tired, but excited about being home, so I only slept for four hours. When I woke, I checked the house's provisions. Felix had kept the refrigerator stocked, but I wasn't hungry yet, so I poured myself a glass of orange juice and walked outside to check out my new digs. The daylight confirmed that the place was in good shape, so I moved on to my pier to check on Simpatico.

My new boat was flashy and it stuck out like a stoplight parrotfish in a school of mullet. It was a little early on a Sunday to be calling people, but I knew that if I wanted to keep the Donzi, I needed to get it out of view, and pronto. So, I called Felix. It took a couple of tries, but finally he picked up and said, "Hola?" I said, "Hi, Felix. This is Jamie." He said, "Where are you?" I said, "I'm in Culebra, at the house." He said, "That's great! I didn't expect you for another week, at least." I said, "I need your help, and I need it right now. Can you bring a trailer big enough to haul out a 43 foot power boat?" There was a long silence and then Felix laughed and said, "Yeah, I think I can manage that."

He showed up thirty minutes later driving a one-ton pickup and hauling a long trailer. We pulled Simpatico out of the water and covered it with several large tarps. Felix and I went into the house and he made coffee. I cooked scrambled eggs and chorizo, and we ate breakfast on the front porch. I told him about the trip from Sarasota and about how I'd acquired the Donzi. Finally, I said, "So, what I need is registration papers and a new paint job. But, there's a problem, I don't have any money." Felix said, "That's not a problem. The paperwork is doable, but it might take a little time. The paint for a boat like this is a little pricey, but I assume that you're going to come to work for me, so we can work something out later. If you help me prep it, I won't charge you for the labor."

Things were turning out great. I'd only been home for a few hours, and I already had a job. I said, "Thank you so much!" Felix said, "Of course, if you want to work for me, you'll have to shave off that scruffy beard." I'd forgotten about the beard. He said, "I have a lot of work for the next two days, but come see me at the boatyard on Wednesday and we'll get started on your boat." I said, "Thanks for getting Dad's Scout running." Felix said, "That was supposed to be a surprise for you." I said, "Oh, it was. Believe me." He mussed my hair and said, "I always knew that you'd come home. I'm glad that it was sooner, rather than later." I said, "My friend Dara and I need to figure out a way to clear customs without having the new boat inspected." Felix said, "Your cousin Clementina is in charge of the customs office here on the island. I'll call her and explain that your sailboat sank before you made landfall and ask her what she wants you to do. I'll call you after I've spoken with her." I was really starting to like this island. We talked for a while longer, and then Felix drove off with my Donzi.

I wanted to fire up the old Scout and take it for a drive around the island, but Dara was still asleep and I was afraid the noise would wake her. Instead, I went into the bathroom and tried to figure out how to get rid of my facial hair. I found a nearly empty can of shaving cream and some old safety razors. The first razor I tried became clogged with stubble and cut into my face. I couldn't find scissors, so I went to the shed to look for some kind of tool that might do for the job. Hanging on a peg board above Dad's workbench, I found an old pair of electric shears. The tines were clogged with what looked like dog hair. I washed the shears off with a garden hose and some dish washing detergent. I carried the shears back into the bathroom, and just because they still smelled a little like dog, I splashed them with some rubbing alcohol before starting on my beard.

After what seemed like an hour, I was finally able to use a razor to trim my beard. I was curious what I would look like with different types of facial hair, so I first gave myself mutton-chops and a goatee. After that, I trimmed it down to just a goatee. The goatee made me look like an evil alternate-universe version of myself, so I trimmed what was left of my beard into a cowboy-style horseshoe moustache. I liked that one, but decided to try something a little more dapper. I gave myself a pencil-thin moustache, but it didn't look right with my shaggy hair. I rummaged around in a cabinet beneath the sink and found some pomade and slicked back my hair with a comb. The effect was rather dashing, and I thought that I could have landed a part in a 1930s Hollywood movie. I didn't have the right wardrobe to complement the look, so I shaved off the last of my facial hair.

I heard footsteps in the living room. The door to the bathroom opened, and Dara stumbled sleepily inside. When she saw me, she jumped backward, raised her fists in a boxer's stance and demanded, "Who the hell are you?" I said, "It's just me! It's Jamie!" She cocked her head to one side and looked me over. Finally, she said, "Huh..." I said, "You obviously miss my beard. I know that it was macho, but don't you agree that it detracted from my manly beauty?" Dara asked, "Jamie, how old are you?" I knew that I'd had a birthday recently, but I wasn't sure exactly how many days it been. I counted the days backward on my fingers until I found the solution and then I said, "I turned seventeen on the day that we sank and raised Eagle Ray, and sailed from Cuba to Inagua." She said, "I trust that you won't tell anyone that I kissed you." I said, "My lips are sealed." She was silent for a few uncomfortable minutes while she stared into my eyes. She seemed to be looking for something. I found myself focusing on her forehead again. I don't know if she found what she was looking for, but eventually she said, "Do you have anything to eat?"

She showered while I cooked her breakfast and tossed her laundry into the washer. She dressed in some old clothes that she'd found in her bedroom. She looked adorable in a 1970s peasant shirt and bell-bottom jeans that had belonged to my father's mother. While she was enjoying my scrambled eggs and chorizo, she said, "So, what's the story with Culebra?" I said, "This is my ancestral home. The economy used to be based on fishing, but now it's dependent on tourism. Other than that, you know about as much as me." She said, "After we square away the Donzi, we should check out the island." I said, "Simpatico has been moved to an undisclosed location where it will undergo a change of identity." Dara said, "That would be a neat trick, for a quarter million dollar boat." I said, "Like I said before, I've got it covered."

After breakfast, we puttered around my property until Felix called and said that Cousin Clementina was waiting for us at Dewey Dock on Ensenada Honda. We took the long route, heading northward up the eastern side of the island. The Scout didn't have power steering or power brakes, or power anything for that matter. But, what it did have was enough low-end torque to pull a plow. It wasn't fast, but it was still a lot of fun to drive. The island looked pretty much the same as I had remembered it. It was your standard tropical paradise, replete with coconut palms, banana trees, and beautiful birds of all kinds. In short, it was heaven.

We passed by a used Catalina 22 with a "for sale" sign hanging from its bow. Dara said, "Slow down!" I stopped the truck near enough to see that the asking price was $2000. Dara said, "You should buy that boat." I said, "That would be nice, but I haven't got any money." It was true that I didn't have any money, but I'd said that just to deflect the suggestion. The sailboat reminded me of my lost lady. Eagle Ray was more than just a fiberglass boat to me, she was a friend. Dara laughed and said, "You're broke, but you're also sitting on a Donzi that you can't sell. I think that counts as irony." She was right. I hadn't thought of it before, because it hadn't occurred to me that I might want to sell the Donzi. When I decided to keep Simpatico, I married that boat. If I tried to sell her, there was a fair chance that I'd eventually get in trouble with the law for not turning her in.

It took us thirty minutes to reach Dewey Station on the western side of the island. We found the U.S. Customs office and presented our documents to Clementina and I wrote down Eagle Ray's registration number, hull number and description on a form that she'd given me. She said, "Jaime, you've grown a lot since the last time I saw you. What was that, three years ago? It's quite a shock." I remembered her from my dad's funeral. I was truthful when I said, "You look exactly the same." She said, "You're sweet. I wish that were true." She completed the paperwork and then said, "Welcome home. I hope that you plan on staying a while." I said, "Prima Clementina, I love it here, and I'm not going anywhere!"

On the drive back to the house, we passed the Benjamín Rivera Noriega airport, and Dara asked, "Does the airport have regular service?" I said, "Yeah, they have daily flights from a couple of the major airlines." She said, "Good to know." That evening, we sat on my pier and fished while we watched the sun go down. We didn't talk much. It was actually kind of nice to feel so comfortable with someone that I didn't feel the need to speak if I didn't want to. I stole a glance at her profile, and felt glad that she seemed serene. I felt guilty about the hardships that Dara had endured because of me. I said, "I've caused you so much trouble. You might have died. At the very least, because of me, you've lost all of your scuba gear." She laughed and said, "Jamie, I hate boredom, and you're definitely not boring. A little bit dumb, maybe, but not boring." I repeated what she'd said to me when I'd told her that I didn't think that she was weird, "That's the nicest thing that anyone has ever said to me." She laughed again, but I wasn't being facetious, I actually meant it.

We spent the next day relaxing, snorkeling and failing to catch fish from my pier. Felix gave me an advance on my wages and so I was able to afford an internet connection at the house and a laptop. We had both been out of contact with our families and friends, so we spent a lot of time composing and responding to emails. I learned that Mom had only received probation. She thanked me for the money that I'd left her and told me that she would pay me back. I told her that the money was a gift, just as long as she didn't ask me to leave Puerto Rico. She agreed to those terms and we arranged for Felix to act as my temporary guardian. So that got me off the hook with the Florida DHS. Mom said that Sarasota was her home and that she was staying. I told her that I would visit.

On Wednesday, Dara and I drove to Felix's boat yard and he showed us to a Quonset hut on the back side of his property. My new lady was inside, resting on wooden struts. Felix gave Dara and me tools and supplies, and we set to work stripping the old gel coat and paint from her hull. By Friday, after three days of prep work, Simpatico was ready for her new face. We could have painted over the old paint job, but she was a Donzi and deserved our best effort.

At the end of the day, Felix inspected our work and said, "Nice job. Now you have a big decision to make. What color do you want me to paint her?" I'd been thinking about the new color scheme ever since I'd decided that Simpatico was mine, almost a week before. I said, "I want the hull to be some shade of white. But, I want vertically slanted, dark orange stripes on both sides, up on the forward quarters. I want it to look enough like a Coast Guard vessel that it discourages pirates. But, I want it to look enough like a civilian boat that it doesn't attract the attention of the real Coast Guard." Dara said, "I like it. It's just like the mimic octopus."

Felix told us that he would take care of the paint job over the weekend and that he would bring my boat to the house on Sunday. We spent Saturday and Sunday snorkeling near my pier and checking out the wildlife. Neither of us felt like eating more fish, so we tried out a few of the local places. Felix and my Donzi showed up on Sunday evening, along with a caravan of vehicles containing all of my extended family. It felt wonderful to be welcomed so warmly by cousins that I'd remembered playing with as a child, and aunts and uncles who I only vaguely remembered. I felt a little guilty that I hadn't learned to speak Spanish better. Every time that I apologized, someone would clap me on the shoulder and say, "You're home now! It'll come back to you soon enough." Food appeared as if from thin air. There were plantains and marinated cassava, and my favorite, cocina criolla. Everyone went crazy over the pork pinchos that Felix had been cooking up on the old brick barbecue.

I felt a hand on my shoulder and when I turned around, I found Carlos Bengoa standing with this hand outstretched. I shook it with both hands and said, "Doctor Carlos! I'm so glad you're here. I have a million questions." He said, "We'll get to them soon enough, but first, let's have something to eat." Dr. Carlos loaded a plate with side dishes, but avoided Felix's grill. He and Felix don't get along. Before sitting down to eat, I introduced Dr. Carlos to Dara, and after exchanging a few pleasantries, Dara returned to a soccer game that she'd been playing with some of my younger cousins. We found a quiet spot and spoke while we ate. I'd been waiting for so long to talk to him that my questions burst forth like water from a fire hose. First, I asked, "Do you know if either of my grandmothers took an anti-viral drug called Gontercon?" Doctor Carlos said, "Definitely not. That drug was found to be unsafe and discontinued before it reached here." I asked, "What do Xanax and Percocet do?" He said, "Xanax is used to treat anxiety disorders. It seems to be effective, as long as the patient doesn't use it along with other drugs. Percocet is a combination of acetaminophen and oxycodone and it is used to treat severe pain. Again, it shouldn't be taken in conjunction with other medications." I asked, "So, you wouldn't prescribe them to treat insomnia?" He said, "Dios mio, no!" He looked around to make sure that no one was listening and then said, "Jaime, you know that because of your condition, you can't take most medications. If you are having trouble sleeping, I can give you a low dose of melatonin." I said, "I'm fine and I'm not taking anything. I was just worried about someone I know who has been taking those meds." I was home, but I was still adapting so I added, "Please call me Jamie."

Our conversation drifted away from the medical field. Dr. Carlos was interested in learning about Sarasota. He said, "I'm going to retire one of these days, and I was thinking about moving to someplace on the mainland. Are there a lot of people my age in Sarasota?" I said, "Yeah, like 95% of the population." He said, "Based on what I have read, it sounds perfect." I said, "I would suggest that you rent there for a while before you make a permanent move." He said, "Really? Why is that?" I didn't want to trash my hometown, but I also didn't want to be responsible for encouraging the man to squander his retirement savings. I said, "It's pricey there and it can be hard to make ends meet. You see a lot of elderly people pushing shopping carts there." His expression read incomprehension so I said, "They have to work those kinds of jobs because they underestimated the cost of living. Doctor Carlos, even working professionals shop at Goodwill. That's how expensive it is there." He said, "That's not a problem. I like to work. If necessary, I will pick up a few shifts at a hospital." I said, "Do what you want, but make sure that you have a bailout plan, just in case you get tired of removing prostate glands." For a second, I thought that he was sneering at me. But, the look disappeared so quickly that I thought that I must have imagined it.

After the festivities had died down and the family had left for home, Dara, Felix and I checked out the Donzi. It was night time, but there were so many tiki torches burning that I could clearly see that the paint job was exquisite. I touched the hull and ran my hand down the length of her. When I reached the aft end of the boat, I found that Felix had painted the name, *Mako* on the transom. I said, "I can see the resemblance between this boat and a mako shark, but I would have liked the chance to name her myself." Felix said, "The name supports your claim to ownership. Five years ago, a Donzi 43 ZR named Mako ran aground just south of Bimini during an offshore race from Miami. She was running at full throttle when she hit, and the forward half of the boat shattered into millions of tiny fiberglass shards. The owner's widow sold what was left of the hull to a salver out of Point Simon on Andros for almost nothing. He loaded her onto a small freighter and hauled her back to his place on Andros. He sold off everything that was salvageable. It took a lot of calling around, but luckily the salving community is a small one. He still had all of the data plates and paperwork."

I said, "So, she's all mine, and it's legal?" Felix said, "It's sort of legal. The story goes like this; I purchased a damaged Donzi 43 ZR from a salver in Andros and sold it to you for...let's say a hundred dollars. You repaired it and restored it to serviceable condition." I'm not normally a hugger. But, I hugged my uncle and said, "Felix, you are the man!" Felix said, "Yeah, I know I'm awesome, but you guys listen up. I checked out this boat's engines, and there are mods that I've never seen before. There are parts on those engines that might have been manufactured one-off just for this boat. They must have been designed by a mad scientist because I have no idea what's going on down there in the engine compartment." He paused for a moment and then said, "Jamie, you can kill yourself with a boat like this if you're not careful. Promise me that you won't open the throttles more than halfway. And only go that fast on glass smooth water." I said, "I promise...unless it's an emergency." I smiled at Dara and she punched me in the arm. She said, "We should have a renaming ceremony." Felix said, "I don't have any champagne, but I do have a cold beer." I was feeling silly a few minutes later when I poured the beer across the bow and said, "Simpatico, your new name is Mako." We knew that we hadn't conducted the ceremony correctly, but Dara and Felix applauded and cheered all the same.

The next morning, Dara and I were eating breakfast when she said, "Jamie, can you give me a ride to the airport in a couple of days?" I like to think of myself as a realist, but when I heard those words I realized that I'd been holding on to the romantic notion that Dara might want to stay with me in my little corner of the world. I said, "Sure, Dara, whatever you need. I was hoping that you'd be able to stay a while longer." Dara said, "Some of my friends from school are renting a cabin near Arapahoe Basin for a few weeks, and they invited me to come stay with them. They say that even this late in the year, there's still snow on the slopes up there. I've wanted to learn to ski since I was a little girl. This is a great opportunity and I can't pass it up." I asked, "Did you buy your tickets yet?" She said, "Not yet. Why?" I said, "The fare will be cheaper if you fly out of San Juan, instead of Culebra. Also, we could take the Donzi…"

I'm not sure why, but when I know that a big change is coming, or that I'm going to be traveling soon, it softens my mood. It was the same with Dara. On Monday, she booked a flight out of San Juan for Thursday and after that she became, almost imperceptibly at first, a little warmer and less guarded. I can't explain it exactly. We spent most of the week playing around with Mako, and when we would take a turn at high speed, she wouldn't fight against inertia, if it pushed her against me. She took my hand, or offered hers whenever we would get on or off of the boat. She walked closer to me than she had before, and put her arm in mine, and it was nice to be so familiar with another person.

The days passed too quickly and before I knew it I was casting off my lines and scrambling aboard Mako as Dara backed off the pier and then headed due east. She took the long route, out past Culebrita and into the Atlantic. She opened up the throttles and we sped across the waves much faster than we should have. Mako cut a swath through the waves, but every time she caught air, the props screamed. Saltwater poured across our bow, into the cockpit, and down into the cabin, but I didn't care. Dara was having the time of her life, and it gave me great pleasure to see her having so much fun. Too soon, we arrived at San Juan Bay Marina.

We took a taxi to the Luis Munoz Marin airport and Dara checked in for her flight. We sat down at a table just outside of the TSA security checkpoint. I said, "I don't know what to say. Except that, I wish you would stay." Charles had told me that when the time came, I should be bold. But, every bold thing that I could think of seemed truculent, petulant or just plain dumb. Dara interlaced her fingers and laid them on top of her head, and then looked around the airport lobby. She puffed up her right cheek and then slowly blew out a long puff of air that pushed her bangs around. Then, she leaned forward across the table, kissed me on my left cheek and said, "Maybe I'll come back around this way next summer." Then, Dara stood up, grabbed her bag and walked away. She breezed through security and headed off toward her plane. She didn't look back.

I took a taxi back to the marina. Mako was running on fumes, but the cash that Felix had fronted me had dwindled, so I only added 20 gallons to the fuel tanks. After settling with the harbor master, I took off. I had to stop the boat several times during the ride back to Culebra. Every time that I thought about Dara, my chest hurt so badly I couldn't safely pilot my boat. The pain would ease up after a few minutes, and then I could continue the trip. I'd never experienced anything like it. During one of the "attacks" it occurred to me to check the refrigerator in the cabin for ginger ale, because Dara would probably say that it would help. It was a random thought, but thinking about that seemed to make the pain worse. I didn't know what was wrong with me. I just knew that I needed to get back to Culebra and see Dr. Carlos.

When I finally made it back to my pier, I didn't haul Mako out of the water like I should have. I just hobbled to my house and dialed Dr. Carlos' number. After several rings, he answered and I described my symptoms. He sounded very concerned and said that I should lie down and that he would be at my house soon. I was lying on the living room couch when he knocked on the front door. I told him to come in and when he did, he was carrying his old-fashioned black leather doctor's bag. He said that it had belonged to his grandfather. Dr. Carlos took my vitals, and as he usually does during his exams, he drew half a dozen vials of blood. He asked me if I'd ever experienced similar symptoms before, and I told him that I hadn't.

Then, he asked me to describe the events of the day. After listening to my description of the previous few hours, he sat down in my Dad's favorite old arm chair and became lost in thought. After what seemed like a very long time, Dr. Carlos said, "I need to ask you some questions which might sound a little odd. Please answer honestly." I said, "Sure, no problem." He said, "Have you ever been in love and have you ever had your heart broken? I mean, when you were living in Florida." I said, "I don't know. I've had a couple of girlfriends. I liked them very much. It was nice to have a pretty girl smile sweetly at me, but there was never anything serious. You know, it was just nice to have someone to go to school dances with."

Dr. Carlos tapped his right index finger against his nose, which was a sure sign that the wheels were turning upstairs. Finally he said, "I believe that your symptoms are a result of your mutation, specifically your over-developed paleocortex. How long were you in close proximity to your friend, Miss Kemm?" I searched my memory for a moment and then said, "We departed

Key West on May 21st and this is June 9th, so twenty days." Dr. Carlos said, "All animals, even the lowly amoeba, secrete pheromones, which are a type of ectohormone that can affect the social behavior of other animals of the same species, and in more complex organisms, between members of the opposite sex. It's a sort of chemically based form of communication. I believe that I mentioned that the paleocortex, which is the phylo-genetically oldest part of the cortical mantle of the cerebral hemisphere, is represented by the olfactory cortex."

I said, "Uh…yes, you have mentioned that my schnozzle is hardwired to the cave-man part of my brain." He said, "The paleocortex might be more accurately described as the reptilian part of your brain. I believe that because yours is oversized, that your brain has become accustomed to the presence of your friend's pheromones, much the same way as a drug addict's brain becomes accustomed to the presence of a psycho-active substance." I said, "You think that I'm going through withdrawal?" Dr. Carlos said, "That's my theory, and I believe that the symptoms will cease within a few hours. It's something of a cliché, but you should probably eat some foods that are high in carbohydrates, or maybe some chocolate. These foods increase the production of serotonin, which will make you feel better." I said, "I feel like I'm having a heart attack and you're prescribing macaroni and cheese?" Dr. Carlos said, "And maybe some chocolate." I said, "You know, I'm more than just a bag of water and chemicals. Maybe I had those chest pains because I'm a romantic and I missed Dara's company." Dr. Carlos shrugged and said, "Regardless of the cause, my prescription is the same."

After Dr. Carlos left, I rummaged around the kitchen and found an old bag of M&Ms. They must have been there for a long time because when I bit into one, I found that the chocolate had turned back into cocoa powder. I checked the expiration date and found that they had expired three years before. I walked out to the shed and munched on the desiccated candy while I fired up the Scout and hitched it to the trailer that Felix had leant me. The candy that I was eating was dry and bitter, but that was the medicine that I'd been prescribed. The doctor's attempt to explain why I was different had always seemed insufficient. I'd asked Felix about the Bonifacio family's arch rivals, the Guzmans and he said that much like our family, most of them had moved away or taken tourism or government jobs. When I asked about Doña Maria Theresa Guzman, he said, "She's still here. She runs a little shop that sells fetishes and charms to tourists. She's crazy and you should stay away from her." Doña Maria loomed large in my imagination. Because my mother had said it was so, on some level I still believed that she really was a witch. Someday, I would speak to her, if only to reassure myself that my condition was physiological and not supernatural.

I pulled Mako out of the water and washed her down. As I went through the maintenance procedures that Felix had taught me, I wondered how many of the people who owned a Donzi actually performed their own routine maintenance. Just tinkering with the beast gave me a great deal of satisfaction, so I guessed that the percentage was fairly high. I'm not normally a sentimental person, or one to treat inanimate objects as though they were people. Still, I just couldn't stop myself from running my hand along her hull as I walked around her. I accidentally smeared a little cocoa powder on the bow. I quickly wiped it off and said, "Oops! Sorry about that." I knew that I was alone, but I still felt a little self-conscious that I'd been talking to a boat. But, I'd started a conversation, so I thought that I might as well finish it. I said,

"Hello, Beautiful. I'm Jamie, your new skipper. Don't worry. I'm

going to take good care of you. We're going to get along just fine.

But, it's important that you remember that you're not a pirate ship

anymore. From now on, you're a salvage vessel."

Epilogue

Those were the events that brought me home to Culebra. The first thing that I did was change my residency from Florida to Puerto Rico. That solved most of my problems, although new problems would soon arise. I enrolled in an online high school and earned my diploma in one year, instead of two. I worked for Felix in his boatyard, and it didn't take long for me to save enough to buy new salving equipment. I sent Zinx photographs of the Donzi's engines, and he sent me back repair manuals and service updates and gave me a link to a forum for Donzi mechanics. Between the two of them, Zinx and Felix were able to figure out how to keep Mako maintained and running at peak performance. Mako has a pretty decent range, as long she's not moving too fast, so I was able to make a little money in my spare time doing some light salvage jobs. The Fensters contacted me several weeks after their return to Naples and asked Felix and me to submit a bid to salve their GT70. They had grossly underestimated the cost of bringing up a sunken yacht, and so we won the contract. Because of that job, I could afford to keep Mako in fuel, and try my hand at treasure hunting.

I wished that Dara was with me, but aside from her absence, life was very good. I'm struggling to find the right words to explain the lessons that I've learned during the trip from Sarasota to Culebra. I didn't learn as much from the things that made me happy, as I learned from the things that caused me to feel regret. I should have been kinder to my mother when I spoke to her in jail and she was in need of support. I should have told Dara how I felt about her during any of the half-dozen occasions when the timing would have been right. But, most of all, sometime during the last three years, I should have bought a bigger boat.

Glossary

Aground: When the hull or keel is touching the bottom

Ampullae of Lorenzini: Electroreceptor organs which can detect electromagnetic fields.

BC: Buoyancy Compensator. A BC is composed of a minimum of four components. 1. Tank bands, which are used to secure to an air cylinder to the BC. 2. An air bladder to which air can be added or vented. This is used to compensate for the compression or expansion of a diver's wetsuit as the diver descends or ascends. 3. A "hard" back plate which can be composed of metal or plastic, or a "soft" back plate which may be made of nylon. 4. A harness which secures the unit to a diver at the shoulders and waist.

Bilge: The lowest interior regions of a hull

BOLO: Be on the lookout.

Cabin Sole: The floor of a cabin

Captain: A Captain is the master of a vessel who is legally entitled to charge for carrying cargo or passengers.

Cetacean: Aquatic mammals such as whales and dolphins

DAN: Divers Alert Network

DM: Dive Master. A DM is a professional-level dive leader. S/he is neither a dive boss nor a diving supervisor. A DM is paid to set the conditions for certified divers to enjoy their own dives. This typically involves a site briefing, a boat ride, and emergency medical assistance, if needed.

EPIRB: Emergency Position Indicating Radio Beacon

Keel: A fin-shaped structure on the bottom of a boat's hull

Lifeline: A wire supported on stanchions around the perimeter of a deck

Lee Helm: The tendency of a sailboat to turn away from the wind

NAUI: National Association of Underwater Instructors

NOAA: National Oceanic and Atmospheric Administration

Olfactory: Relating to the sense of smell.

Ozone: A molecule composed of three Oxygen atoms. O_3

PADI: Professional Association of Diving Instructors

PFI: Performance Freediving International

Sea Anchor: A canvas drag used in deep water to prevent drifting or maintain a head-to-wind orientation.

Sheet: A line (rope) used to control the alignment of a sail

SDI: Scuba Diving International

SSI: Scuba Schools International

Skipper: A skipper is the person who has been determined to be in charge of a vessel. The word "Skip" is of Scandinavian origin and means "Ship Boss." A skipper may only charge passengers if he or she is a licensed captain.

STCW Certification: International Convention on Standards of Training, Certification and Watch-keeping for Seafarers. A certification required of anyone serving as a crewmember of a merchant vessel or passenger ship.

Tiller: A lever that is used to control the angle of a rudder and thereby steer a boat.

Six-Pack: A Captain's license that authorizes the holder to captain a boat carrying up to six passengers

Sloop: A sailboat with one mast, a mainsail, and one headsail (jib).

Weather Helm: The tendency of a sailboat to head up into the wind

Jamie Will Return in: *Mako*

67785666R00157

Made in the USA
Charleston, SC
21 February 2017